Black Widow's Bite

Book One of Monsters in the Darkness Series

Bella Reves

Contents

List of Trigger Warnings

- Drug Use

- Alcohol

- Burning/burns

- Drowning

- Mentions of Self-Harm

- PTSD

- Explicit Sex

- Described Blood

- Mentions of Death

- Mentions of Suicide

- Mutilation

- Torture

- Violence

- Kidnapping

- Swearing

- Snakes

- Spiders

- Stabbing

- Suicidal Ideation

Dedication

Family are the ones you choose,

and the ones who choose you.

Chapter One

Addison

Today just felt wrong, and it was putting me on edge. It felt similar to how it felt when the music changed in a horror movie, and you just knew that something terrifying was about to happen. The weird feeling started because of a dream, the same one I've had every night for the past three weeks. I felt like I should've technically classified it as a nightmare, but somehow, even though it would make Freddy Krueger himself say 'Whoa, tone that shit down', I couldn't exactly consider it a nightmare, per se.

Every night it was the same thing. It began as soon as I fell asleep, and it never changed. I was walking down some stairs to a creepy basement that I didn't recognize. The walls were old, and chunks of the drywall had crumbled, or maybe rotted away. There were no lights on in the basement, and as I groped around in the dark, I managed to stumble and fall into a large pit. It felt like I was falling forever, and when I finally reached the bottom, I landed on a giant spider web. Dream-me should really just stop wandering around and stay safe and sound on the web, but instead, I climbed off and continued down a long tunnel. Snakes were slithering all around my feet, hissing, as I narrowly avoided stepping on them. There were so many of them that it looked like the entire floor was moving by the time I reached the small room at the end of the tunnel. When I entered the room, I saw a man sitting on a throne of skulls, a crown of scorpions encircling his head. Blood was dripping down his face from where the scorpions had stung him, but the man was smiling, beckoning me forward. As I approached, I saw that in the spaces where his eyes should have been there was a horrible, gaping darkness. Smoke began to pool out of the holes, and he laughed as my skin caught fire, burning and crackling as it spread over my body, consuming me entirely.

That was normally the part where I woke up, sweating and tangled in my bedsheets like I'd tried to physically run away from my subconscious. This morning had been no different, and I groaned when I checked my phone and saw it was only 5:30 a.m.—over an hour before my alarm was set to go off.

I ripped my sheets off and hopped out of bed, knowing from previous nights that I wouldn't be able to fall back asleep. Instead, I showered and dressed, watching the sun slowly begin to filter in through my window as I got ready for the day. It wasn't quite autumn yet and, even if the lab stayed cool with the A.C., it was still decently warm outside, so I grabbed a black blouse and a pair of grey slacks out of my closet. I pulled my pitch-black hair up into a casual bun, opting for function over style, as usual. Since I was so early, I decided to walk to campus instead of bussing, which I normally did in the mornings to facilitate a few extra minutes of sleep.

I was hoping the fresh air would help me shake off the last dregs of the dream. Maybe it was the exhaustion talking, but I couldn't get the nagging feeling of impending disaster out of my mind, even after I reached the University science building. The campus was still half-asleep, and I had to turn the light on once I reached my department, the first one to arrive this morning.

Most of the time, dreams were simple enough to interpret. They were, after all, just a collection of data that your brain collected over the course of the day and was committing to long-term memory as you slept. But this dream made no sense to me. I've never had a particular fear of heights, or snakes for that matter. I wasn't religious, so the weird devil-man was pretty off-topic with respect to what I normally got on my mind. As for the spider web, well...

I scanned my key card when I reached the lab and turned on the lights to illuminate the hundreds of spiders and scorpions that filled the room in tanks of various shapes and sizes. The Arachnology lab had been my home-away-from-home for the better part of five years, ever since the second last year of my entomology degree. Currently, I was working on my Masters' thesis in Arachnology, so it would've actually been weirder if spiders weren't appearing in my dreams at this point.

Since there weren't a lot of people who felt like dedicating their lives to hanging out with spiders, I had my own little office inside the lab. I turned on my office light and dropped my bag on the floor before plugging in the coffee-maker in the small communal kitchen area at the back of the lab. I yawned and stretched as I watched the liquid-energy drip into the pot, pouring myself some before it was completely finished brewing. Settling into my office chair with my mug, I continued ruminating about the dream plaguing my nights, while my computer screen blinked to life in front of me. I really should consider it a nightmare, but the problem was that no matter how creepy and irritating it had been, I just... wasn't frightened by it. The themes practically screamed trauma, especially the burning alive part. I knew all too well what fire felt like when it licked across my skin. Touching the collar of my blouse instinctively, I smoothed down the fabric, running my fingers over my chest and along my collarbone, tracing the scars hidden underneath. The fire in my dreams didn't hurt, not like real flames, at least. It was a different kind of heat, one that had me waking up with an ache between my legs and a physical need deep in my core.

So... not quite a nightmare, although it did speak volumes about my love life—and mental health—if I was getting turned on by a smoke-eyed dream demon. If I were a believer in such things, I would have said that this wasn't a dream or a nightmare, but an omen, and a bad one at that. It would explain why I couldn't get rid of the foreboding feeling that had my teeth on edge. My grandmother used to say that the feeling was caused by someone stepping onto your grave. If she had been still alive, she would've read way too much into my dream. Instead of coffee, she would have had me drinking some horrible, homemade herbal tea that could have supposedly protect my soul from the devil. No doubt, I would have been sleeping with lavender under my pillow and lining my window sills with salt. I missed that crazy old bat and her superstitions. They'd really livened up an otherwise depressing childhood. I'd never really believed that killing a spider in the house would bring rain, or that you didn't speak the names of the dead, else their spirits would be drawn back to the world. I've always been a pretty big skeptic, which was funny, considering I could kill people just by fucking them.

I didn't kill them outright. It's not like we were having sex and they suddenly dropped dead of a heart attack mid-thrust or anything. In fact, there was nothing about their deaths that could even be linked to me. I'd read hundreds of studies, done hours of research, and still hadn't found one single shred of scientific evidence that explained why every person who had ever so much as kissed me had either gone insane or died horrifically within days of it happening.

It started all the way back in the fourth grade, when Kevin Vanbrite kissed me on the lips at recess. A week later, he'd been moved to a special school after he pulled out and ate all of his hair. During a game of spin-the-bottle at a high school party, I'd made out with Tyson Grant. Two weeks later, he'd been admitted to a psychiatric facility, having suffered a psychotic break due to what they thought was early-onset schizophrenia. Heather Detante and I went to second base on a dare, during a sleepover later that year, and she'd overdosed on her mom's pain medication and spent our senior year in a coma. A few rumours had started about me by then, so my love life effectively dried up until I moved away to college.

After one too many beers at a frat party, I'd ended up losing my virginity in the back of some guy's car. The act itself hadn't been that memorable, but seeing him on the news only two days later was—apparently he'd walked in front of a train. Back then, I thought it was still a random set of horrible coincidences. But after two more hook-ups ended abruptly and violently—on their part—I couldn't ignore the common factor any longer. For whatever reason, my touch made people crazy. So, for the most part, I stopped touching people.

I was not a bad person, and I didn't want to hurt anyone. However, I figured out, through careful trial and error, that just a small amount of skin-to-skin contact could encourage people to do things for me. If my fingers brushed against the baristas as they handed me my coffee, suddenly I didn't need to pay for it. A quick handshake, and now my apartment was $300 less a month. A graze of my skin, a little prompt or 'nudge', and an interaction I was having would lean in my favour. I figured it was my cosmic right. If I couldn't get laid, I could at least get a free coffee or two. Nobody was getting hurt by that, right?

Despite the horror movie vibes surrounding me like a menacing shroud, I managed to get through my day at the lab without anything going horribly wrong. That was a good thing, since my work was centred on highly venomous spiders. Usually, I had the whole place to myself, only crossing paths with two other faculty members over the course of the day. I didn't have any friends on campus, or really, anywhere, for that matter. It was hard to be close to someone when you could hospitalize them with a hug. I was polite with my colleagues but distant, and eventually, everyone I met just got into the habit of leaving me alone.

I was beginning to feel the lack of sleep when I finally called it quits for the day. The walk home was a lot busier than it had been earlier this morning, and I had to actually pay attention to avoid bumping into anyone as I trekked down the sidewalk. Restaurants were already starting to fill up with happy hour guests, and I dodged around groups of smokers on the sidewalk as I tried to make it back to my apartment.

My gaze focused ahead of me, I nearly tripped as something ran under my feet, scampering across the sidewalk. I caught myself before I ate shit on the pavement and watched in disbelief as a small black cat bolted into a nearby alley. My grandmother's voice echoed through my head, screaming at the glaringly obvious omen. I walked over to the alley entrance and spotted the cat sitting on the dumpster, eyeing me cooly, as if I'd tripped over it on purpose. I'd noticed a lot of stray cats around here over the years. Most were the result of students, who adopted them when they came for school and then abandoned them when they graduated and moved on. They seemed to live well enough on scraps and whatever mice I was sure lived here as well, but I always felt bad for the orphaned felines. It wasn't their fault their owners left them behind.

I fished around in my purse until I found a small can of tuna. I always kept one or two in my bag now, just in case I found someone who looked particularly hungry. Plus, if this little creature was a bad omen, maybe feeding her would get me back into the cosmic good graces. I opened the can carefully so I didn't spill any of the liquid on my slacks, and I set it down beside the dumpster. The bad omen stared at me for a moment, assessing my motives, and then jumped down gracefully and started sniffing around the can. Once she began eating, she seemed to relax somewhat, and I crouched beside her to give her a few gentle scratches behind her ears. Looking past her into the alley, I caught a glimpse of something strangely familiar behind the dumpster. Letting curiosity get the better of me, I moved closer until I could make it out. There was a set of stairs leading down from the alley to a dank and unlit doorway.

Nope, fuck that. I'd seen enough horror movies to know how that would end. I backed up immediately, colliding with something behind me in my haste. Spinning around, I realized there were now two scruffy-looking men blocking the entrance to the alley. My bad omen hissed and took off, and I didn't blame her. I wanted to do the same. Instead, I just squared my shoulders and gave the men a casual but detached look. "Excuse me, fellas," I said, going to side-step around them. The one closest to me shifted to block my path, and I took a quick step back before he could touch me.

"What's the rush, sweetheart? We just want to talk for a minute." He sneered, his gaze sliding over my body. His buddy snickered, and I saw a flash of metal in his hand—probably some kind of weapon, with my luck.

"I've got thirty dollars and a granola bar. Take it," I told them, dropping my purse at their feet. In reality, it was more like twenty dollars and some restaurant coupons, but they didn't need to know that. My heart sank when they stepped over the purse, clearly not their intended target. I didn't want to hurt anyone. I truly didn't. But hey, they fucking started it.

The big one, who'd called me sweetheart, grabbed for me again, his hand latching onto my wrist where my shirt sleeve had ridden up. "Let me go," I told him firmly. "I'm not worth it, trust me."

His grip tightened for a moment, then loosened, and I snatched my arm away from him. "Fuck this, she ain't worth it," he muttered to his friend and made no further effort to grab me. His friend gave him a confused look, but didn't seem deterred by his sudden change of heart. Thug number two lunged at me, and I tried to dodge him, but he caught my shoulder, and I fell back, slamming into the brick wall behind me. He held up the knife, snarling at me like an animal. As soon as he was close enough, I attacked, dragging my nails down the side of his face. He howled in pain, blood oozing from the gouges I'd left across his face. In my victory, I briefly let my guard down, and he struck out suddenly, backhanding me across the face. The force was enough to knock me sideways, and as I stumbled for footing, the ground abruptly disappeared underneath my feet. It was at that moment I remembered the set of stairs I'd been trying to run away from. Fate had decided I wasn't allowed to escape them after all, evidently. I landed roughly, the concrete steps knocking the air from my lungs as I tumbled my way to the bottom. I felt my head smack against something hard, and then the world around me went dark.

CHAPTER TWO

Wyatt

I heard the aging metal groan in protest as I crawled out onto the fire escape, and I dared it to give way. The three-story fall probably wouldn't kill me. At most, it would make for an interesting end to an otherwise dull-as-shit day. I sat down on the side of the fire escape, facing the street, ignoring more creaks as I shifted to dangle my legs off the side. I cracked open the beer I'd brought up with me, sipping it as I listened to the noises of the street filter down the alley I was currently presiding over.

The view was shit, but I was at least high enough so the dank smells of garbage couldn't reach me. A spider crawled across the rusted-out railing in front of me, probably out searching for dinner like the people on the street below us. I wouldn't eat until later, most likely, if at all. Piper was supposed to get groceries this week, but he'd been on one of his benders since Monday and hadn't gotten to it. We still had beer at least, so that was something. Maybe I could steal his phone and order something for us. He always had a credit card or two loaded in his apps—all of them stolen, of course.

Piper's kleptomania was an ongoing problem that we had yet to solve, but it did come in handy occasionally.

The tattoo studio was closed for the day now. I'd only booked two sessions this afternoon, and the last one had finished early. We didn't advertise for walk-ins. In fact, we didn't technically even have a storefront. At one point, there had been a sign that said 'Tattoos' above our door, in sad neon letters, but it had been knocked down during a bad hailstorm, and we hadn't bothered to replace it. The only way people knew how to find us was by booking an appointment through the website I'd set up. Once it was confirmed, I sent them the address, and only then could they find me and the studio. Apparently, being hard to find actually made us appear cool and mysterious, so we haven't had any complaints as of yet. It was better this way. We didn't need people popping in unexpectedly. That almost always ended poorly, or violently.

I sipped my beer, my head resting against the railing as I surveyed the activity on the ground below me. Catching movement at the mouth of the alleyway, I watched one of the local cats slink toward the dumpsters. We had tons of them around, but as long as they kept to themselves, I didn't mind. Sometimes I could hear them fighting during the night, usually over a mate or a territorial dispute. Their yowls would filter in through the windows, and the next day I'd find some blood or tufts of fur. The alley was like the kitty version of the Wild West.

Someone else caught my eye, and I shifted to get a better look, lowering my sunglasses down to the bridge of my nose. A young woman walked into the alley, her eyes fixed on the very same cat that I'd been watching. Finally, something potentially interesting was happening. The woman looked like a professional of some kind, with nice clothes and fancy hair. She was definitely too nice-looking to be hanging around here. She must have had an eclectic friend who'd lured her here for a night out or something. She took something out of her purse and set it down for the cat—a tin of food it looked like. Who the fuck walked around with cat food in their purse? Maybe she wasn't so fancy, after all.

Before I could dwell on that question, I noticed two men had stopped at the mouth of the alley, eyeing the woman with consideration. I finished my beer in two gulps, crushing the can in my hand. I didn't like the look of this. Something about their stance was too predatory to ignore. She hadn't noticed them yet, her attention shifting to the staircase leading to our building's basement. I wondered what would possess her to do that since it was probably the most uninviting location in the surrounding area, purposefully might I add. As I'd anticipated, her good sense had her backtracking out of the alley, only to run into the two men I'd been worried about.

Sure enough, the big one tried to grab her, blocking her path to prevent her from escaping. I shifted into a crouch. I knew I couldn't make the jump without breaking my legs, but I could swing down the busted ladder in a pinch. The woman threw her purse—a good move, but unfortunately not what they were interested in. I snarled and tossed my can down, preparing for the jump I was about to make. Then, something strange happened that made me pause. The big man grabbed her wrist, and whatever she said just... stopped him dead in his tracks. Even after his friend lunged at her, he didn't move and looked dazed, like he'd taken a punch or two to the head. An inhuman howl got me moving again, and I scampered down the ladder, jumping once I reached the last rung. I rolled when I hit the ground, springing up in time to see the woman fall backward down the stairs, landing in a heap at the bottom.

My heart plummeted, and rage took over as I pulled my knife out of my pocket and jabbed it into the side of the guy who'd thrown her. He let out a string of curses as he shoved past me. I wrenched the knife out of him and let him go, blood staining his jacket as he hauled his dazed friend with him out of the alley. *Good, let him bleed out somewhere else.* It was less likely it could be linked to us then.

I waited until I was sure they'd gone and ran to the stairs, jumping down to the bottom where the woman lay unmoving. It looked like she was breathing, but I couldn't tell much else in the dark recesses of the stairwell. Thankfully, I kept my keys to the building in my pocket so I wouldn't have to drag her around to the front door. I unlocked the basement door and carefully scooped the woman up into my arms, being respectful of her personal space as best I could and avoiding the areas where her clothes had torn. This was a terrible idea, but the alternative was leaving a potentially dead woman on our doorstep, and we definitely didn't need that kind of attention.

CHAPTER THREE

Addison

I felt like I'd been hit by a bus. As consciousness slowly began seeping back into my brain, I became uncomfortably aware of all the different body parts that were hurting, and I wasn't a fan. I had a brief thought that maybe I was dead, but I would think death wouldn't hurt this much. More of my awareness filtered back, and I realized I wasn't in my bed at home. I also wasn't on the ground, which was where I vaguely remembered ending up after falling down the stairs. So where the fuck was I?

I opened my eyes, blinking as the light set off a pounding in my skull. I touched the side of my head where it was hurting the most, and my hand came away red—well, that wasn't ideal. Sitting up slowly, I discerned that I was lying on a worn-out leather couch, but the where was still unknown. I was still wearing my work clothes, although my blouse was ripped at the shoulder, and one knee in my pants had torn. Nothing seemed broken at least, but my ankle felt sprained. I must've hit it in on a step on the way down. I could almost hear my grandma chiding me for ignoring the bad omen, the

I-told-you-so dancing on her lips with a sad smile. She didn't like it when I got hurt, but that old bat just loved to be right.

As my eyes adjusted to the lighting, I examined the room some more. A run-down pool table was on one side, next to a beer fridge and a bar counter. An odd collection of lounge chairs, a futon, and the couch I was lying on sat haphazardly around a crooked coffee table. Judging by the tiny windows along the top of the wall, I had to be in some kind of basement. A shiver went down my bruised spine. Maybe this was what was behind the door at the bottom of the stairs I'd fallen down.

A noise made me jump, and I saw a quick flash of someone standing in the nearby doorway before they disappeared from view. Yeah, I needed to get out of here. This was starting to feel a little too much like a horror movie. I stood up gingerly and tested putting weight on my feet. My left leg was fine, but when I tried stepping down on my right foot, a stabbing pain went through my ankle, and I stumbled, catching myself on the couch. Fuck, I'd have to hop my way out of here, apparently.

"You should sit down for a minute. You hit your head pretty hard," a gentle voice announced. I whirled around, still standing on my good leg, trying to look more threatening than I currently felt. A guy—roughly my age, if I had to guess—was standing by the door, holding a bottle of water in his hands. He had shaggy dark hair that fell in messy waves around his face, and dark aviator sunglasses that must've made it difficult to see down here, in the dim basement light. I couldn't tell much about him. Other than him being relatively tall, the giant black hoodie he was wearing obscured his shape.

"I'm actually going to get going now," I told him sharply, looking behind me toward the door. If I hopped quickly and didn't trip, I could probably make it there before he could get around the table.

"I'm not one of the guys who jumped you," he said softly, holding his hands up. "You're in the basement of my tattoo studio. I saw you fall and didn't think you'd appreciate waking up in a pile of mouse shit." He took a step toward me, hands still raised. I tensed, but let him step closer, and he set the water bottle on the table in front of me. He seemed harmless enough, although only douchebags and psychopaths wore sunglasses inside, so I didn't quite trust him.

I waited until he backed up again and took a seat in the furthest chair from me, then I grabbed the water off the table. The lid was still sealed, so I didn't think he'd tampered with it. I took a long couple of drinks while he watched me in silence.

"Well, thanks for the water, and for, uh, finding me, I guess." I smiled thinly. "I am going to leave now, though." I took a step toward the door, stumbling again as my ankle refused to hold up. The guy was out of his seat and reaching for me faster than I would've guessed he could move. Flinching away from his hands, I grabbed the nearby chair for support. "I'm fine," I snapped.

"You're clearly not," he replied evenly, but backed away a step. "Why don't you let me take a look at your ankle and make sure it's not broken?"

"Listen, *Shades*, I appreciate your help, but you're not a doctor," I bit back. "So just keep your hands off me and let me leave." I took another hop-step toward the door, my eyes on him as I used the chair as a crutch.

"My name is Wyatt, and how about we make a deal? You can dial 9 1 1 on the phone and hold it the whole time I check your ankle. If it is broken, you can just hit dial and call an ambulance," he offered. He pulled out his phone—*oh fuck, I wonder where my purse had ended up*—and dialled the numbers, holding it out for me to take.

He was being semi-reasonable, so it was hard to argue without seeming like a lunatic myself. At least, if he was trying to kill me, he was making it a lot harder for himself. I kept my eyes on him as I snatched the phone and sat down on the chair I was gripping onto, propping my leg up on the rickety table. Wyatt walked over slowly, like he was trying not to spook a wild animal, and sat down on the edge of the couch, close to my leg. I lifted up my pant leg, exposing my ankle and my shin. It was definitely bruised and starting to swell. He reached out to touch it, and I flinched away.

"You said you were going to look," I reminded him sharply, and even with the sunglasses on, I could see the exasperated look in his eyes.

"Listen, *sweetheart*, I can't tell if it's broken, unless I check around the bone. I'm not just trying to feel up your ankle," he replied sarcastically. He was frowning at me, probably trying to figure out if my lovely personality was God-given or the result of brain damage from the fall.

"My name is Addison, not sweetheart. How about I feel around it, and you tell me what I'm supposed to look for?" I snapped back and started pressing gently around the part that was swelling. Wyatt sighed heavily and shook his head.

"Alright, fine. Does anything move that shouldn't move when you push on it?" he asked. I felt around, wincing when certain points stung as I prodded them. I shook my head. Nothing was moving, at least.

"Great, can you wiggle your toes?" he asked me next and waited while I tried. I nodded, all toes accounted for. "Okay, then I think you just sprained it. Is your car nearby? I can help you get to it," he offered. I pulled my pant leg down and sighed.

"No, I was walking home from work. I live nearby... ish," I added, cringing slightly. Well, now he knew I lived close, so I was really making it easy for him to hunt me down and kill me. He looked at me for a moment—probably thinking about how best to stuff my body in a dumpster.

"My, uh, roommate has a car. He'll be home later tonight. I could drive you back to your place then?" Wyatt suggested. I really didn't want to stay here any longer than I had to, and my hesitation must have been a good enough answer. "Okay, well, I have something that could help take some of the pain, so you could limp home on your own then."

Awesome, I loved that my options were hanging out in a stranger's creepy basement or taking sketchy pain relief from a stranger. Today was really living up to its potential.

"Sure, what is it? Like numbing cream or ibuprofen?" I asked. Anything, just to get out of there at this point.

"Not exactly," Wyatt replied, running a hand through his messy hair. "Can you just let me touch your ankle for a second? It'll help, I swear."

Okay, what was his deal? Was there an ankle fetish society I was unaware of? I glared at him.

"Not a chance, *Shades*, I will give you one last warning. Do not touch me. Trust me, it's not worth it." My skin prickled uncomfortably, thinking about the two men in the alley. I wondered if I'd see either of them in the news later this week, dead from a self-inflicted injury.

"What exactly did you do to that guy in the alley?" Wyatt asked me abruptly, like he could hear what I'd been thinking, and my eyes widened. Had he been watching the whole time as those men attacked me? "He touched your arm and then just stopped. Why?" He was leaning forward now, clearly interested. I didn't need him interested. I needed him to leave it the fuck alone.

"I told him I had a gun," I lied, poorly it seemed, because he just brushed it off with a shake of his head.

"No, because the other guy kept coming, the one you didn't touch. What happens when people touch you?" Wyatt pressed, leaning closer. He was like a bloodhound who'd caught a scent, and I was the cornered fox.

Why was he so insistent on this? Most people just wrote off the weird shit that happened around me as unrelated accidents. Aside from the rumours in school, no one had ever put together the connection, so why had he? I didn't like to be cornered, especially by some douchebag wearing sunglasses in a dark basement.

"Try it and find out," I snarled at him. He cocked an eyebrow at me, and his arm shot out, hand hovering above my calf, just above my bruised ankle. I swiped out a hand of my own and knocked his stupid glasses off his stupid face. They landed on the couch, and we both looked at them before looking back at each other. Wyatt's eyes were black, not dark brown, but pitch black. He had no irises that I could see. It looked as if it was just a pupil sitting in the centre of the whites of his eyes. As I stared, his pupils grew, spreading out until both eyes were completely black. The world tipped, and I felt myself falling into the blackness.

CHAPTER FOUR

Wyatt

I had tried to do the right thing, and nevertheless, I'd managed to royally fuck it up. I shouldn't have brought her inside in the first place, but I had this nagging feeling in my gut that there was something weird about her. Addison was not the high society chick I'd thought she was when I'd first seen her. Sure, she dressed the part, but I recognized a scrapper when I saw one. She was just hiding behind a mask of normalcy. I expected her to get a bit cagey when I tried to touch her leg, I was a stranger after all. I hadn't expected her to slap my glasses off, though, so we were both caught off guard when her consciousness tumbled headfirst into mine.

Some of the weirdness in my life I could control with a bit of effort. I didn't go around kidnapping people's minds very often, so I was a bit rusty at this whole thing. I closed my eyes and sank down into myself, following Addison into the part of my mind that seemed to exist solely as a holding cell for anyone who decided to make eye contact with me.

"Addison, can you hear me?" I asked. I got back a lot of noise and emotions, mostly rage, and I winced. "Look, you're the one who knocked my glasses off. I didn't do this on purpose. Can we just talk for a minute, please?" If she was listening, she'd be able to hear the truth in my voice and feel the sincerity in my words. I waited until the storm of anger subsided and took that as a yes. "As you can see, I've clearly got something a little freaky happening in my life. All I want to know is, what happens when someone touches you?"

I braced myself as a deluge of memories crashed over me, pummelling me with images of people screaming, a kid missing chunks of hair, and a house burning down. Loneliness, fury, and fear mixed together, threatening to drown me. That was enough of an answer for me.

However it worked, I pushed her mind out of my mental holding cell, shoving it back out where it belonged. I averted my eyes, using my hand to shield them from Addison while I groped for my glasses on the couch. I heard her gasp as she came back into herself, and I braced for the explosion.

"What the fuck did you just do to me?!" Addison yelled, putting her hands to her face as if reassuring herself that it was still there. I gave a small shrug, running my fingers through my hair. She looked like she would happily bite off my ear and spit it back in my face. "Don't you dare shrug! What was that?!"

"Honestly, I don't know." I held up my hands defensively. "Just like how you don't know why you make people crazy." I grabbed her abandoned water bottle off the table and finished what was left inside, feeling more than a little drained after that experience.

Addison was speechless for a moment, gaping at me with a look of murder in her eyes. "You can't just- I don't know who you are- how fucking dare you-" I couldn't help but smile as she struggled to find the right thing to yell at me. Her hair was coming undone from her bun, creating a halo of darkness around her face.

I got up and walked to the makeshift bar we had set up in the corner and grabbed a half-empty bottle of vodka off the counter. I opened it and took a swig straight from the bottle, enjoying the burn as it coated the back of my throat. Walking over to the couch, I held the bottle out to her, which stopped her mid-rant. After a moment's hesitation, she snatched it out of my hand and took a large swig of her own.

"So, do you want me to fix your ankle, or what?" I asked, reaching for the bottle back. Addison stared at me incredulously and took another swig before passing it to me.

"Are you out of your fucking *mind*?" she demanded. "Of course you are. And I am, too. Jesus, I should've never followed the damn cat." She groaned, dropping her head in her hands. Okay, I wasn't sure how the cat factored into things, but she'd clearly had a long day, so I didn't comment on it.

"Bear with me here, what's the worst-case scenario? I go crazy and jump off the roof?" I shrugged again. "That's a regular Tuesday evening. Either way, you get to leave." I handed her back the bottle, and she took another drink. I waited, hand poised at the ready.

"Fuck it, whatever. I tried to warn you." Addison sighed, throwing up her hands in defeat and slouching down in the chair. Well, this should be fun. Gently, I placed my hand above her ankle, just brushing against the swelling. We both held our breath, waiting for something to happen.

At first, all I noticed was a distinct humming sensation running from her leg up through my hand, like I was grounded but touching a live wire. The lights in the room seemed to brighten, and I felt warmth flood my body like I was standing out in the sun. So far, so… weird, I guess. I focused my attention on the swelling and tugged at it with my mind. Slowly, along with humming, I could feel the pain and the inflammation creep into my hands and up through my arms. I shivered as the pain finally settled into my own ankle. I noticed that the humming had gotten more potent, and I let go of her leg to sever the connection. The feeling was sharp and abrupt through my entire body, a horrible emptiness that left me both numb and raw at the same time. It felt similar to the crash after a high. My skin itched with the need to touch her again.

"Jesus," I muttered, sitting back on the couch. Addison had been studying her ankle, which was significantly less swollen now. She took one look at my face and handed me the vodka.

"So?" Addison asked tentatively. "You're the first person I can ask about this. You can't hold out on me now, Shades." I smiled wanly, taking a small drink. While I was settling myself, she stood, testing her ankle. When it held her weight, I thought for a split second that she would make a break for the door, and the thought made me desperately sad. Instead, to my relief, she just sat back down, waiting for my answer.

"I don't think you're driving people crazy, like breaking their minds or anything," I told her finally, the vodka starting to bring the warmth back into my limbs. "I think it's more like… you're a drug. When they can't have more of you, they can't handle the withdrawal." I let that sink in as I took another drink, and she gestured for the bottle. Handing it to her, our fingers brushed, sending a shock of intoxicating warmth through my body again. I resisted the urge to grab her hand as she pulled away, and the feeling faded, leaving me aching once more.

Addison took a long drink, shaking her head sadly. "It makes sense, I guess," she murmured. "It would explain why the longer I touch someone, the worse it seems to get." She sank back into the chair. "This whole time I just hoped I was crazy."

"You'll fit right in with my friends," I told her quietly, noticing Austin slipping into the room. "We're all mad here."

CHAPTER FIVE

Addison

I didn't know if I could handle much more weirdness today. I had never told anyone about my unusual problem before, and honestly, I had planned on taking it to my grave. But I guess who better to talk to about it than a guy with scary black eyes who can read my mind? We were like a two-person support group for freaks.

Wyatt shifted a bit in his seat, and I noticed he was favouring one of his legs when he moved. "Addison, this is my friend, Austin. Don't worry, he's cool. He's, uh... like us, I guess," he told me carefully. I looked over and noticed a guy—Austin, I assumed—standing near the door, his eyes downcast.

"Hey... Austin." I gave a little wave. "I'm Addison, you guys can call me Addy, though." I gave Wyatt a nod. I'd say my friends called me Addy, but I had no friends, so... "We're just having a drink. Want to join?" I guess I might as well lean into the crazy. At least, now, with three people, it could really be a support group.

Shit, I might be a little drunk, or in shock. Probably both.

Austin shot a surreptitious glance at Wyatt, who nodded back at him. Quiet as a mouse, he joined us, sitting down in the chair furthest from mine. Unlike Wyatt, who was dressed for some kind of snowstorm, Austin was in a faded tee shirt and jeans. His hair was blond, nearly white, the sides cropped short while the top was left long, and he had it slicked back, away from his face. At first glance, Austin was deceptively slim. It was only when he got closer, I could see that he was all muscle on a slender frame. His hands and arms were covered in tattoos that were made to look like patches of green scales poking up from under his skin. He had a small gold hoop in his eyebrow, and several more in each of his ears. There were two hoops on his bottom lip, one on each side. Along with all the piercings, he also had thick snake-skin bracelets coiled around both wrists. He kept his eyes downcast, and Wyatt wiggled the vodka at him enticingly.

Austin snatched it from him and took a long swig, then levelled his gaze at me. His eyes were entirely golden-green, the pupils narrowed into black slits. In a normal situation, they could've been some truly impressive cosmetic contact lenses, but since today was already an absolute horror show of weirdness, I put money on them being real. I stared back at him evenly, holding out my hand for the bottle. A ghost of a smile tugged at the corners of his lips, and he passed the bottle across the table. It was nearly empty now. We'd managed to drain it pretty quickly.

"Alright, what's your angle? Do you read minds, too?" I asked, raising an eyebrow as I rested my elbows on my knees, leaning toward him.

"No," Austin whispered. He had a raspy quality to his voice, like he wasn't used to using it. "I just do the piercings here."

Wyatt and I both burst out laughing, mainly at the ridiculousness of the situation, but I was sure the vodka contributed, as well.

Austin finally cracked a smile, and I saw that his top two canines were longer and thinner than the rest, more like fangs than human teeth. One of his bracelets started to wiggle, and I realized with a start that they weren't just snake skin, they were actual, real, live snakes. The little red-and-black-striped snake uncoiled enough to peek its head out, testing the surrounding air with his forked tongue. Austin stroked it absently, his own tongue poking out to play with his lip ring. A slight flare of heat ignited in my core.

Okay, no more vodka for me tonight. Which was fine because Austin finished the last of it, anyway. Wyatt got up and limped over to the bar in the corner, still favouring his leg, and I heard bottles clinking as he rummaged around behind me. When he returned, he had shed his oversized hoodie, and I'm not ashamed to say that I openly gawked.

The man was deathly pale, like he had never seen the light of day, but there must've been a gym in whatever cave he lived in, because his whole body was toned under the ratty, black tank top he was wearing. What shocked me the most were his tattoos. Black whirls covered his arms and what I could see of his chest and neck in no discernible pattern. They reminded me a bit of those Rorschach tests psychologists made you look at, to see what your subconscious would find in the patterns.

He held out a beer, which I accepted with a small nod, hoping my jaw hadn't actually dropped open in shock. He tossed another beer at Austin, who caught it effortlessly and cracked it open immediately.

"Cheers, mate." We all glanced up as a third man walked in, snagging the beer out of Austin's hand before he could take a sip. The man stood in front of us and chugged the beer in one shot, then crushed the can against the side of his head and tossed it over, toward the pool table.

Wyatt sighed and jerked a thumb at the new guy. "That's Piper." Piper looked over at me, noticing me for the first time. He appeared normal enough at first glance, and by that I meant there weren't any horns coming out of his head. His eyes were a decidedly normal blue, but the way he was looking both at me and through me was unsettling. His chestnut hair was cut fairly short, and it was currently messy from sleep. He was shirtless, and I didn't see any tattoos on him, on his upper half at least. The jeans he was wearing were sitting low on his hips, showing off the deep V of his trim stomach.

Piper crossed his arms over his chest, tapping a finger on his chin thoughtfully. He had dozens of leather and rope strands around his wrists, covered in an assortment of trinkets, some of which made a little tinkling sound when he moved his hands. He had nearly as many necklaces, all handmade, using seemingly random materials. "What day is it today?" he asked. "I thought you were coming on Tuesday." I shot a confused look at Wyatt as Piper wandered over to the fridge, grabbing more beers. He tossed a new one at Austin, opening a second one for himself.

"Sorry?" I asked, confused. "You must be thinking of someone else. I ended up here by accident," I explained.

"No, no." Piper shook his head emphatically. "I saw this, for sure. On Tuesday, a little black cat will drop a black widow on our doorstep. It looks dead, but it's only playing." He winked. I couldn't figure out what his accent was. Something European-sounding for sure, but I couldn't tell what.

"Piper is a fortune teller," Austin told me quietly, holding his new beer closer to his body for protection.

"Like a palm reader?" I asked, and Piper looked deeply offended.

"Absolutely not," he huffed, dropping down beside Wyatt so that he was next to me. I shifted my legs, narrowly avoiding his as he propped them up where mine had been. "I listen to the world, and when I listen right, I hear whispers. Sometimes I can even send out a whisper of my own." He smiled wickedly.

It was no longer feeling like bad luck had brought me here today. Something made me wonder if Piper had whispered to that cat from earlier today, telling her to trip me and lure me into the alley. I took a swig of my beer and sat forward, glaring at him. "Have you been making me dream weird shit for the last month?" I asked coldly. Wyatt and Austin both stiffened at the word dream, and I didn't need to be a mind reader to interpret that.

"I don't make dreams." Piper waved a hand. "But I've been feeling this tug lately, a string in my chest, like calling to like. I just..." He shrugged. "I tugged back, I guess. I don't know what happens from there." Great, he was fucking crazy. I looked at Austin, who just shrugged and sipped his beer, then at Wyatt, who just looked tired.

"Have you guys had dreams, too?" I asked quietly. "About a demon with smoking eyes?" Piper snorted a laugh, and Wyatt slapped him on the chest. "What?" I demanded.

"Well, he's not actually a *demon*," Wyatt replied quickly, "But it kind of sounds like you're describing a friend of ours. He owns this place." He pointed upstairs.

"Who thinks I'm a demon?" a voice asked, and I looked toward the doorway, dark now that the sun had gone down. I saw the outline of a person, with eyes glowing like burning embers in the shadows.

CHAPTER SIX

Cain

I fucking hated banks. It was my name on the damn business license, and my name on the damn building title, so that meant every time there was some kind of error, or paperwork went missing, I had to haul my ass out to the bank and straighten it out. My hands curled into fists as I clenched the steering wheel, and the smell of burnt plastic wafted up to my face.

I put on the suit and tie and played at being civilized and complacent until I thought my face would crack in half and fall off. If I wasn't responsible for feeding three other idiots, I would've burned the place down on my way out. The low thrum of a headache was starting at the back of my skull, and I grimaced.

And that was another thing. Why the fuck was I responsible for *them*? Everything had been just fine when I'd been on my own. Well, fine was a bit of a stretch, but fucking simple, at least. Then Piper had wandered into my life and, despite my best efforts, wouldn't leave me the fuck alone. He had proved useful, though. We stumbled our way into some good fortune that had nabbed us the building, which I couldn't have done on my own. But then fucking Austin had slithered out from whatever rock he'd been hiding under half his life and found his way to our place. And just when I'd gotten him sorted out, Wyatt had appeared out of nowhere, half-dead and nearly catatonic from severe depression.

I didn't want the responsibility. I didn't need it. All I wanted was to be left alone.

I grabbed a cigarette out of the cup holder and stuck it in my mouth. It lit up with a spark of red as it touched my lips, and I inhaled deeply, letting the smoke pour into my lungs. It was a terrible habit; I knew that. But most of the nasty shit burnt up before it could do any damage to my already fucked up system, anyway.

I pulled into the only reserved stall we had at our building. Fuck the customers. They could park on the street somewhere. I was the only one who actually had a car, anyway. The others just borrowed it when they went out for something. I went through the front door and continued up the stairs to the apartments above the studio. This building was a weird old design, with a store area on the main floor and a living space above. The kitchen, bathroom, and my room were on the second floor; Austin, Wyatt, and Piper had their own rooms on the third floor. It was a good-sized space, as long as Piper didn't dream anyone else into our lives.

The suit came off immediately, and I tossed it in a heap on the floor. I grabbed a pair of sweats and pulled them on, contemplating just trying to get some sleep. I couldn't sleep at the best of times, plagued with a variety of nightmares that I'd had since I was a kid. Lately, I'd been having a different sort of dream, one that Piper had insisted wasn't because of him, but I didn't believe him. Every night for nearly a month, I would dream about being caught in a spider's web. No matter how much I kicked and thrashed, I couldn't get free; it would only draw the attention of the spider. It was person-sized, absolutely enormous, with a jet-black body and a red stain on its back. Every night, it would crawl across the web toward me, and once it reached me, it would jab its pincers into my throat. I would wake up gasping for air, still feeling like teeth were pressing into my neck. For some reason beyond my understanding, I would always be rock hard. I'd never felt an attraction toward anything with more than two legs in my life, and I wasn't exactly loving the murderous spider, but my body seemed to have other ideas. Maybe it was some fucked up fear response, Fight or Flight or Fuck, I guess.

Not ready to face the spider just yet, I wandered back to the kitchen to check the fridge. Of course, Piper hadn't picked up the fucking groceries. I grimaced, searching for a beer at least, but they must've all been downstairs. I slammed the door shut and headed down, hearing voices floating up toward me from the stairs. It was a little unusual to hear all three of them up and talking. Austin was normally holed up in his room, and Piper had been on another one of his drug-induced journeys. When I left this morning, he'd been unconscious on the floor. Wyatt, well, he'd had clients today, so I knew he was up and about, but it was usually pretty tiring for him, so I was surprised he hadn't crashed yet. I observed from the doorway for a while, listening to the sounds of something close to normalcy emanating from the room. We didn't approximate normal here, not by any stretch. I bristled, fists clenching. Whenever we tried for normal, someone got hurt. It wasn't safe for anyone, and I wasn't ready to put one of these idiots back together again.

My ears perked when I heard Wyatt mention me. "Who thinks I'm a demon?" I asked, and the room went silent. I stepped into the light, scanning the room. Someone new was there, an unusual sight for sure. We didn't have guests over. The longer people were around, the more likely it was they would start to notice some of the weirder aspects of our little rag-tag group. And it was not like we had any family who would drop by for a visit.

"Hey, Cain." Wyatt cleared his throat. "This is, uh, Addy. She had an accident on our steps. I brought her inside to... uh..." he trailed off, noting my expression.

"An accident, huh?" I looked the girl over cooly. She looked pretty comfortable right now, but I did spot the torn pant leg and the rip in her blouse, which probably weren't cosmetic, judging by the scrapped red skin underneath the black fabric. She sat up in her seat, meeting my glare with a level gaze.

"Some guys jumped me, knocked me down the steps," Addy explained. We stared at each other in silence for an uncomfortable length of time, and I stalked further into the room, joining their little circle of chairs. No one was dumb enough to make a sound, and Addy's mouth hardened into a thin line. I gave a little nudge, just a small burst of heat, and I saw her cheeks flush at the sudden warmth. Her eyes narrowed, but she didn't break eye contact. She was a stubborn bitch, I'd give her that.

As usual, Piper was the one to finally break the silence, either oblivious to the tension or simply bored with it. "It's Tuesday," he told me as if it was a brilliant piece of news. I dragged my eyes over to him, levelling him with a look.

"I fucking know it's Tuesday, Piper. What of it?" *God help me.* I couldn't take his cryptic shit some days. Storming over to grab a beer out of the fridge, I noticed we were getting low on those, too. Well, if anything got him sobered up enough to shop, it would be a lack of beer. I grabbed the remaining free chair and sat down, still eyeing the girl—Addy—with suspicion.

"I told you." Piper sighed as if I were the exasperating one. "The cat is coming today to drop a black widow at our door." I grimaced at him. He must've thought he'd told me this nonsense already, but half the time he just hallucinated the conversations. I would've remembered something about a black widow. It sounded too much like my dream he claimed to know nothing about.

"Wyatt, I should get going," Addy announced unexpectedly. For a moment I thought I saw a pained look cross Wyatt's face, and I suppressed a groan. I couldn't have him falling for someone again. He was in such a funk for months the last time that I just barely pulled him out of it.

"Why?" Piper asked, and Addy looked surprised.

"I have to get home. I work in the morning," she explained gently as she stood.

"How's your ankle?" Wyatt asked, and I saw her flex one of her legs out experimentally. "Are you sure you don't want a ride?" He stood up as well, chivalrous all of a sudden, and he appeared to be avoiding putting weight on his one leg. I narrowed my eyes suspiciously, and he avoided meeting my gaze, deliberately ignoring me.

"It's a lot better now, thanks." Addy smiled at him, and he seemed to glow under the small bit of praise. "I'm fine walking home. It's not far." Christ, this was a nightmare.

She walked to the basement door, which we rarely even used, and everyone's eyes followed her. See, this was why we didn't have people around. These idiots got too attached too quickly, and then they got hurt. She gave them a small wave, ignoring me completely, and disappeared out the door. The air seemed to follow her out, leaving a void of sadness in her wake. Even the lights seemed to dim once she was out of the room, and Wyatt shrank down in his chair, seemingly deflating into himself.

I huffed and stood up, following her outside. I had to put a stop to this before it got too out of hand. As I approached, I caught her searching the ground of the alley, squinting in the darkness. I heard her let out a small victory cry when she found what appeared to be a bag beside the dumpster, crouching down to dig around inside it.

Stalking up behind Addy, I tried to look as menacing as possible, which wasn't hard. According to Wyatt, I looked menacing most of the time, anyway. This was one of the many reasons I didn't interact with the clients who came by the studio. I waited quietly while she fished through the bag and pulled out a set of keys. She straightened and yelped when she finally noticed me behind her, her hands closing into fists. "What do you want?" she snapped at me, brushing her hair out of her eyes.

"You're planning on walking home, alone in the dark?" I asked incredulously, looking out at the nearly empty main street. On the weekends, some bars stayed open late, but it was a weekday, so most everything was closed by now.

"Of course. I do it all the time." Addy straightened, settling her purse over her shoulder. I took a step closer, looming over her, and she crossed her arms over her chest defensively.

"Aren't you scared?" I asked, my voice dropping to barely above a whisper. Fear was a good thing. It kept nice people inside with their doors locked, safe from all the freaks and the things that went bump in the night, like us.

"Not in the slightest." She smirked. I waited for her to step away, but she held steady, and I had to admire her stubbornness. Too bad it was being directed at me. I pulled a cigarette out of my pocket and stuck it between my lips. The cherry flared up in the darkness, and her gaze fixed on the red glow, the light reflecting in her eyes. I exhaled the smoke through my nose.

"You shouldn't come back here," I said finally, my voice pitched low enough so anyone eavesdropping wouldn't hear.

"You're probably right," Addy replied, before turning on her heel and walking away. I gritted my teeth, watching her leave. I had a feeling that regardless of my warning, she was going to do whatever the fuck she wanted.

CHAPTER SEVEN

Addison

No dreams woke me up early this time. In fact, I somehow overslept. I rolled over with a groan, a dull ache throbbing behind my eyeballs thanks to the vodka last night—although, I was sure falling down the stairs hadn't helped much either. Strangely enough, my ankle looked almost completely normal, like nothing out of the ordinary had happened. There was just a minor bruise left from my fall, the only visible evidence I hadn't just hallucinated the bizarre encounter last night.

I got dressed in a hurry, slipping on a navy blouse and a pair of black jeans today, since my nice slacks were now in need of mending. Brushing my hair quickly, I opted to leave it down. There were hair ties on my desk, if it started to irritate me later. I still couldn't believe my purse had still been there when I'd left the studio last night. I thought for sure I'd be hunting down my landlord at midnight for the spare key. Everything was still inside, even my wallet and my phone. Maybe the black cat had felt bad about getting me jumped and had watched over it for the evening. Honestly, it wouldn't be the weirdest thing that happened in the last twenty-four hours.

As I walked to campus, I couldn't stop thinking about the mysterious group of men I'd met last night. I'd missed the bus, thanks to my late alarm, but at least the weather was still mild this morning, and my ankle didn't hurt, which was a plus. As I walked past the alleyway, I glanced up at the building where they supposedly worked. It looked vacant at first glance, most of the windows blocked out with newspaper. I thought I could see the shape of a man standing out on the fire escape, but the sun was shining in such a way that I couldn't make them out. Cain's threat, or warning, although it had felt like a threat, still echoed through my head. He didn't want me around, and that made me angry, because for once I had met people who I had something in common with. Wyatt had given me more answers about myself than I'd ever had before. I wondered if I'd see his name in the news sometime soon, and I hoped that I wouldn't. If he knew what it was, maybe he wouldn't succumb to the madness like everyone else. Or, maybe, he was already too mad to be much affected.

Work passed by in a haze. I drank several cups of coffee and tried my best to make a dent in the methods' section of my research. My shoulder was starting to twinge where I'd scraped it on the pavement, and I rubbed it idly while I reread a paragraph in my notes for the fourth time in a row. Someone knocked on my door and my head shot up. "Come in?" I called, frowning. No one ever stopped by my office. Maybe there was a fire drill?

The door opened with a creak, and a man with mousey brown hair and round glasses popped his head in. I recognized him immediately. Pete was the researcher working with a few species of scorpions and had the office space next to mine. "Sorry to bother you, Addison." He smiled nervously. "I was wondering if you'd seen any… well… any snakes around here?"

I blinked at him, assuming I'd misheard. "I'm sorry, what?"

"A couple of the grad students told me they'd seen a snake loose in the department. We have a few people looking around, but I just wanted to check and see if you'd, uh, seen it?" I looked behind him, trying to see if there was a group hazing going on. He was alone, and I had a sinking feeling this wasn't just a coincidence. Pete was watching me nervously, as if I might lunge at him. I'd never been particularly rude to him. Maybe he just had a nervous constitution.

"Someone in the Zoology department is probably panicking over their missing research project." I laughed, and Pete lightened up with a smile. "I haven't seen any snakes here, but I'll be sure to scream if I do." Giving him a polite smile, I stayed frozen as he nodded at me and shut my door. I waited a beat to make sure he was gone and then quickly looked under my desk. Nothing. Checking the other side of my desk, nothing slithered into view there either. Great, not only was I crazy, but I was also full of myself. Not everything weird that happened on campus had to do with me.

Getting up, I went over to the coffeemaker to freshen up the cold dregs left in the bottom of my mug. When I grabbed the pot, I saw a small tail disappear behind the machine, and I nearly dumped the coffee in shock. I quickly put the coffeepot back on the machine and moved the entire unit over to the side. There, curled up over a water stain, was a small garter snake. I looked around to make sure no one else was nearby and held out my hand tentatively. The snake uncoiled and slithered into my palm, wrapping itself around my wrist with a light squeeze. Coffee forgotten, I walked back to my office before anybody came out and witnessed me charming a snake.

"You don't belong here, do you?" I whispered to it after my door was safely shut and locked. I lifted my wrist so I could look it in the eyes. It, being a snake, did not answer me, and I felt ridiculous. What the fuck was I supposed to do with a snake? It seemed cozy enough wrapped around my wrist, but I couldn't just walk around campus with it. My reputation as the aloof spider lady was bad enough. I didn't need to give people any more reason to pay attention to me. Giving the snake a little pat, I sat back in my chair to think. Technically, I was done with my in-lab work for today anyway, and it was not like my hours were being logged anywhere but in my thesis journal. I packed up my books, careful not to jostle my little tag-along, and locked up my office.

"Heading home for the day?" Pete piped up, and I jumped back from my door, bumping into him in the process. He grabbed my elbow to stop me from falling, his hand brushing against my bare skin. Fuck, I'd rolled my sleeves up to avoid getting pen ink on them and, with all the snake nonsense, I hadn't bothered to fix them.

"Sure am, have a nice day," I told him kindly, quickly pulling out of his grasp. His eyes were glazed over, and he looked confused. I felt a moment of guilt, hoping he wouldn't be too affected by the brief contact. Hiding my other arm behind my purse, I turned and left the lab as quickly as I could manage without actually running. Luckily, I made it off campus without bumping into anyone else.

When I reached the tattoo studio, it still looked abandoned. I tried the front door this time, and it was unlocked, so I let myself in. The main floor of the building looked similar enough to other tattoo studios I'd seen, except it was missing a storefront. There was a side table set up near the door, with a credit card scanner on it. That must be the front desk. There was no seating or waiting room of any kind, just a hallway leading to a couple of rooms with tattoo chairs and tools. One of the doors was closed with an 'Occupied' sign on it, so I left that one alone for now. I looked over at the stairs going up to the second floor, and my living bracelet moved its head to look up as well. I took that as its way of saying "Go that way", and headed upstairs, ignoring the 'Do Not Enter' sign taped up on the wall.

The second floor opened into a small kitchen area, with appliances that would've been in their prime back in the 90s. A shabby-looking table with four mismatched chairs sat in the centre of the room. A door down the hallway creaked open just as I was peering up the stairs to the third floor, and Cain appeared in the hallway, looking murderous. Great, of course, I just had to run into him. He must've just woken up. His reddish-blond hair was adorably messy, which was a sharp contrast with the scowl on his face. He was holding his shirt, just about to put it on, and I caught a glimpse of some wicked-looking scars covering his chest before he pulled his shirt down to hide them. Cain ran a hand through his hair to smooth it down as he stalked toward me, his lip curled up in a snarl.

"Was I not clear last night?" he demanded, his voice rough from sleep. "You're trespassing now. This is private property." He stopped just short of me, looming over me like I was supposed to cower before him. I held up my arm, revealing the snake on my wrist.

"Does this guy look familiar? I found him in my lab today," I replied tartly. For a split second, he looked genuinely baffled before his mask of anger slipped back down.

"You experiment on snakes in a lab?" Cain asked, frowning, and I rolled my eyes. *God save me from the stupidity of men.*

"No, I don't experiment on snakes. But I think someone here might be missing a snake, and I came to return it. Trust me, I'm not here to see you," I snapped and moved to head up to the third floor. Cain stepped in front of me, and I gave his chest a frustrated shove. His hand wrapped around my wrist before I could flinch away, and I watched the rage on his face melt away into confusion. His grip was white hot, and I felt heat seeping up my arm, a flush rising on my cheeks. I tried to pry my wrist away from his hand, but he had a grip like iron. Fuck, this wasn't good. I yanked at my arm, but Cain seemed frozen on the spot, gaping at me like I'd grown a second head. I gave his chest another shove with my free hand, but he didn't move. In desperation, I slapped him hard across the face, and that knocked him back a step and loosened his grip enough for me to slip away.

He was still staring at me, but with a renewed intensity I'd never seen before. He took a step closer to me again, and my breath hitched, but he didn't try to touch me at least. I was still warm from his touch, and the heat was starting to build somewhere a lot lower than my arm. Cain was looking at me like he wanted to devour me, and it was terrifying because he was obviously unhinged, but oddly sexy as well. I think I needed to get my head examined, either by a shrink or by an M.D., maybe both. I took a step back, but he closed the distance immediately, warmth radiating off his chest.

"How the fuck did you do that?" he asked hoarsely. I opened my mouth to answer, but the words died off in my throat. I tried to take another step, but my back hit the wall, and he had me pinned. For the second time in two days, I had the overwhelming sense that I was about to die in this building.

Chapter Eight

Austin

You wouldn't really think it, but snakes actually had an amazing sense of smell. Mine wasn't as good, but it was a lot better than most people's, and I could smell Addy as soon as Wyatt had brought her into our home. I'd watched her for a bit while she was on the couch. Wyatt had asked me to keep an eye on her while he rooted around for some bandages in the kitchen. She was pretty, I guess, although she didn't have many piercings. Just two in her ears, like a lot of women seemed to have. She smelled amazing, though, with a similar undercurrent of sharp spices Wyatt, Piper, and Cain had. It was that dark spice what marked her as different, just like us. I hid again when she woke up, choosing to listen from the shadows as she and Wyatt talked. He was good at the talking part. He had to be because his job took longer than mine. I just stabbed people and got paid. I preferred it that way.

We never had people over. Piper said it was because we were unsettling. When Wyatt got in one of his moods, he said it was because god had forgotten about us, and people didn't like that. I didn't need the company of people anyway, so it didn't make me sad. But I'd been so curious about the girl who smelled so good that when I heard Wyatt explaining things to her, I figured it might be safe to join in. Addy had looked right at me, and she hadn't been scared or disgusted. She'd just looked at me like you would anyone on the street. This was what it must have felt like to be normal. I enjoyed listening to her talk, watching as her hands moved, noticing how her tongue poked out to lick her lips after she took a drink.

I was so disappointed when she'd had to leave. Why couldn't she stay? We all had, after Piper had called us here. I didn't think Cain liked her much. He didn't like anybody, though—sometimes I didn't even think he liked Piper. Wyatt told us after she left that her touch was dangerous. She was like a drug, and we had to be careful about it. He looked like he wanted to touch her more. He always liked drugs, though. Drugs didn't always work right for me. Sometimes I could feel something, and sometimes they just made me tired. I wondered if touching her would make me tired, or if I would feel normal, like I did when she looked at me. Piper called her a spider, but she didn't have fangs. I had checked when she smiled. Maybe they were just hidden and slid out only when she was close enough to bite.

I had opened my window a crack this morning, letting the smells of the street waft into my room. I waited all morning, hoping I could catch her scent. She said she lived close by, and she worked someplace she could walk to, so maybe she would walk past us again. I waited and waited at the window, curled up next to my heating block. It was mid-morning when I finally caught a whiff of her on the breeze. It was faint, but unmistakably Addy. One of my friends slithered over to the windowsill to check it out with me, and I whispered to him in a language only we knew. I asked him to find out where she was going and keep her safe for the day. My friend slipped out after her, and I waited by the window until I couldn't smell her anymore.

Eventually, I wandered out of my room to check the fridge, but Piper wasn't back with the groceries yet. I didn't go out much, unless it was late, otherwise people would stare at me. Wyatt wore sunglasses to hide his eyes, but I didn't like wearing them very much. They made it too difficult to see. Piper was lucky. People didn't mind it when he went outside and walked around. He would even visit the farmer's markets on the weekends when he wasn't too stoned to get up, and he made extra cash telling fortunes. He told me that a lot of the fortunes he gave out were bullshit, but occasionally, someone would come along and he'd feel a little extra about them. Those people would often come back and see him again later in the studio.

I had a couple of clients booked in today, two septum piercings back to back. Septum piercings were in style right now, and most of the people who wanted them didn't have any other piercings yet, which led to problems. I've had a few fainters and a few people who panicked when they saw the needle. I tried to calm them down as best I could, but people rarely felt at ease around me, so it didn't seem to help. Today, at least, both girls were excited to get them done and managed not to faint in the room. They took a lot of pictures though, which I didn't like, and they even asked to take a picture of me. I said no politely because Wyatt told me we needed good reviews to keep up business. One of the girls seemed to want to talk to me a lot, and she slipped me a piece of paper with her number on it. I tossed it in the trash after they left. She smelt sour, like the tang of curdled milk, and I didn't like that.

After I cleaned up my tools, I wiped everything down with a pungent antiseptic wipe that cleared away the smells of the clients. It was so strong it plugged my nose, and I didn't realize until I was already halfway up the stairs that Addy must've been nearby. I had heard a commotion upstairs, but I had assumed it was Cain in one of his dark moods and dismissed it. I bounded up the steps and nearly crashed into both of them.

"You came back," I whispered, ignoring Cain. He seemed mad about something, but he was usually mad. I saw my little friend wrapped around Addy's wrist—he'd not only found her, but he'd brought her home! I grinned broadly, and Cain moved back, still looking weird. Addy smiled back at me, holding out the hand where my snake was coiled around.

I forgot Wyatt's warning in my excitement and brushed my hand against hers as I reached out for my friend. My skin buzzed like bees had crawled into my bloodstream, and her smell enveloped me completely, making my head spin. I was only distantly aware of the snake slithering over my hand and up my arm. When she pulled her hand away, the feeling dissipated immediately, leaving an aching emptiness in my chest. Letting out a small whine, I reached for her again without thinking, wrapping my hand around the back of her neck. I coiled around her, pressing as close as I could and burying my face against her neck so I could inhale her scent. Addy squeaked as my other hand wrapped around her waist so she couldn't move away again. I shuddered, nuzzling against her neck where I could feel her heart racing. My body was responding in a very human way, and I pressed against her, making her gasp, her hips moving against me. My teeth grazed along her neck, and her breath hitched, her scent getting stronger, threatening to drown me.

I was never letting go of her again.

Chapter Nine

Wyatt

I've walked in on a lot of weird things living here with these guys. There was the time Cain had a violent fit and nearly melted all the kitchen tiles, his clothes burning away to cinders when I walked in. Then there was the time Austin hatched a nest of vipers in the bathroom sink, and everyone had to piss in the alley until he wrangled them all back into his room. Piper liked to meditate naked on the kitchen table, so that was almost expected at this point. I had never walked in on Austin trying to kill someone though, that was new.

I'd been trying to sleep off the hangover from last night, having no clients booked to come in today. I successfully wasted the morning away dozing, but some loud shouts and a crashing sound had me throwing on a shirt to go downstairs. Cain was the one shouting, which wasn't a shock. He tended to be the loudest of us. He was trying to pry Austin off of Addy—shit, when had she come back?—but it clearly wasn't going well. Austin had his hand on the back of Addy's neck, which explained enough.

"Cain, try not to touch her, okay?" I warned. "No offence, Addy, but we don't need two people jumping on you right now." I circled them, seeing Austin's face pressed into her neck. She was up on her tiptoes. He was holding her so tightly, he was starting to lift her off the ground.

"We need to have a talk about that," Cain growled at me, and I waved him off impatiently. Addy's face was a mix of emotions. Her cheeks flushed and her lips parted. Austin was pressed flush against her in a very intimate manner, which wasn't how we normally treated the people who came to visit us.

"Can you try to move?" I asked her quietly, and I watched her put her hands on his sides, pushing away from him hesitantly. He made a keening sound low in his throat and gripped her tighter. I saw her shiver as Austin rubbed his face along her neck, his teeth flashing as they brushed over her skin. His eyes closed and his face looked blissfully happy. I rubbed a hand over my face, stuck on what to do.

"Just turn it off," Cain snapped, and she shifted to glare at him.

"You think I do this on purpose?" she hissed, and Cain raised his eyebrows, caught off guard. She reached up and ran her hand over Austin's neck. "Hey Austin, it's okay. I'll stay for a while. But you need to put me down. You're scaring your friends," she murmured, and he whimpered a little before relaxing his hold, the hand along her back dropping off so she could set her feet back down. I took my chance and stepped between them, breaking his contact with her. Austin snarled, his teeth snapping at me, but Cain already had his arms around him, lifting him off the ground and pinning him so he couldn't bite me.

Addy was leaning back against the wall, catching her breath. I might've imagined the flash of disappointment that crossed her face, but it was quickly replaced by concern. "Is he going to be okay?" she asked me. "Why did he react like that?"

"I'm not sure, but I've seen snakes do similar things." I shrugged. "He's different, so he reacts… differently?" I wasn't much use in this department. Now that she was so close again, my fingers itched to touch her as well. It was like trying to quit smoking with a lit cigarette in the room.

"What the fuck are you?" Cain demanded, his voice strained as he continued to hold Austin off the ground. Austin, for the most part, had calmed down, but now he just looked sad. Cain set him down on the floor but didn't let go, in case he tried to lunge at Addy again.

Addy just sighed. "What the fuck are you?" she countered. "Besides an asshole." Cain was momentarily stunned, which was an impressive sight to see.

"I told you, her skin is like a drug. Normal people get a pretty bad withdrawal from it. Some even offed themselves," I explained, running my hand through my hair.

"You seem okay though, from yesterday?" Addy offered, but it sounded more like a question.

"I still feel it there. It's a nagging sensation, but I can ignore it," I told her gently. "It's like the best kind of high. Everything is brighter, more in focus. I crave you like a fix." She blushed a deep red, and I realized that was a very loaded comment. I cleared my throat and looked down at my feet awkwardly.

"That's not what it felt like to me," Cain announced, and I looked at him in surprise. "It made everything quiet. All the noises in my - just, everything got peaceful." He glared at me, daring me to make a snarky comment. I wasn't about to touch that. I liked my eyebrows un-singed.

"You smell so good," Austin whispered, "You feel like... *home*." Cain let go of him slowly, but he didn't make a move toward Addy, just looked at her despairingly. Addy shifted on her feet, her eyes moving between us.

"I'm sorry. I wish I knew how to turn it off or pull it back somehow." Addy rubbed her arms anxiously. "If I could even dilute it so it wouldn't drive everyone insane..."

Austin was moving toward Addy slowly. He probably didn't even realize he was doing it. I moved in front of her, cutting into his line of sight.

A noise on the stairs startled all of us, and Piper clomped up, his bracelets clinking together as he hauled several bags of groceries up the stairs. "What's with you lot?" he asked, dumping them all in a heap in the kitchen. He eyed Cain and Austin and gave a little smirk. "Everyone's had a taste I see," he mused. "While the cat's away, the mice have an orgy, eh?"

"Austin got a little overwhelmed," I told him shortly. "It seems to affect him a little more than us." I put a hand against the wall, blocking Austin as he tried to creep around me to get to Addy.

"The longer the contact, the worse it seems to be," Addy explained. "I'm really sorry. I should just leave. Maybe that will help a little." She moved toward the stairs, and Austin lunged, nearly knocking me down the stairs.

"Please don't leave again!" he begged, eyes wide. "It feels good just having you close." He quit struggling against me once she stilled. I thought about it, and he was sort of right. The itch to touch her was there, but I felt lighter now than before she'd arrived. I was more clearheaded for sure. I looked at Cain, who was frowning, deep in thought.

"So it happens even when you're not touching me?" Addy asked, looking to me for additional confirmation. Austin wasn't the most reliable source of information at the moment. I nodded, and Cain gave a quick nod as well, clearly finished with his own self-assessment.

"Well, now I'm just feeling left out," Piper mused, his nose crinkling in annoyance. He swept past Austin and me, and before I could stop him, he put both of his hands on Addy's face.

"Do you mind, love?" he asked coyly. Addy gaped at him, and he swept her into a kiss.

Chapter Ten

Addison

I was just trying to return a pet snake, and suddenly everything got very complicated. I practically lived the life of a nun, and now very attractive men were touching me a lot, and it was all getting a bit overwhelming.

Piper came out of left field. I was still busy watching out for Austin when he grabbed me, and before I could tell him what a terrible decision he was making, his mouth was on me. Fuck, I'd forgotten how good it was to kiss someone, especially someone who knew what they were doing. Piper took my parted lips as an invitation, and he tipped my chin up, his tongue sweeping into my mouth as he deepened the kiss. Heat pooled between my legs, and I was getting dizzy from the sudden lust that swept through me. It had been so long; my skin craved the touch.

Piper pulled away after a moment, leaving me breathless. His pupils were so dilated, he nearly matched Wyatt's, and it seemed to take a lot of effort for him to let go of my face. "Well, that is something," Piper murmured, touching a finger to his lips. "You taste like the clouds." I didn't know what he meant by that, but seeing the hunger in everyone's eyes as they stood around me made me blush.

"I think we all need to just chill out for a second," I breathed.

"I need a fucking drink," Cain announced and walked past us and down the stairs. Piper rummaged through the bags he'd brought in, tossing Wyatt a case of beer and grabbing a bottle of rum. The rest of the groceries lay forgotten on the kitchen floor. I followed after Piper, feeling a little numb, and I heard Wyatt and Austin right behind me.

Cain was already chugging a beer when I got downstairs, and I sat across from him on the couch. Piper opted for the chair closest to me, leaning back and taking a long swig out of the bottle of rum. I guess these guys didn't believe in cups. Wyatt sat Austin down on the opposite side of the couch, sitting beside him like a babysitter, cracking a beer to hand to him. Piper offered me the bottle, and I took it gratefully, sipping the brown liquor and focusing on the burn as it slid down my throat.

"You should've never come back here," Cain muttered, and I bristled, shooting him a glare.

"She had to come back," Piper said, before I could say something nasty back at him. "She felt the tug." He poked his chest as if that somehow proved it.

"Technically, it was a snake," I corrected him, taking another drink before I handed the bottle back. I felt the couch dip and noticed that Austin had shifted closer, still drinking his beer.

"Cain, come on. You can't deny that this is... not an accident." Wyatt sighed. "What did you say it was?" He looked at Piper. "Like calls to like, or some shit like that." He threw up his hands.

"I didn't mean to cause any trouble," I told Cain sharply. "Not only did I not ask to get thrown down the stairs, I also warned you all not to touch me. I never wanted to hurt anyone." I closed my eyes and pinched the bridge of my nose, frustrated in several ways now. Somehow, I'd ended up responsible for the lives of four different people, and it was a lot of fucking pressure. Something brushed my arm, and I opened my eyes to find Austin right next to me. I touched his hand gently, and he seemed to instantly relax on the couch. I held his hand, so at least one person here could chill the fuck out.

Cain grimaced, but apparently, he didn't have a good retort, so he just crushed his empty beer can and tossed it aside.

"So listen, the reality of things is that I'll need to leave at some point," I told them, and felt Austin tense beside me. "I can come back though," I finished quickly. "But I have work. And my own apartment..." Fuck, my list was actually painfully short.

"You could bring your things here," Austin piped up, playing with a strand of my hair. "You could have this room!" He said it so matter-of-fact, I almost laughed.

"I can't move in here. I only just met you." I smiled, and his face dropped.

"All in good time," Piper mused, and I narrowed my eyes at him.

"No more of that shit now," I told him sharply. I didn't think I could handle any more of his twists of fate this week. He just shot me another coy smile, his eyes flashing with a hunger that made me shiver. He handed me the bottle of rum, and I took a sip to cover my reaction before passing it back. Austin's hand had drifted to the back of my neck, tickling his fingers lightly along my hairline. His touch was not helping me think clearly at all.

"I need to think," Cain announced, slapping his hands on his thighs and pushing himself to his feet. He jerked his head at Wyatt as he walked past, and Wyatt gave me a quick nod before disappearing after him. Piper just chuckled and took another swig of rum, closing his eyes as he tipped his head back to rest against the chair.

Well, alright then, I think I was slowly starting to understand the bizarre dynamic of this group. I shivered as Austin started to nuzzle against my neck like he had earlier, the cool metal of his lip rings tickling behind my ear. I felt his breath against my skin, and *my* breath caught in my throat when his tongue darted out to trace a line up under my jaw.

"You taste so good," he murmured into my ear, and his hand tangled in my hair, pulling my head back gently and exposing my neck. A small moan escaped my lips as he began trailing kisses across my throat, his tongue lapping against my skin. This was a bad idea, I knew that, but it felt so good. Austin put his hand on my leg, and I shifted myself up and over to straddle his lap. He buried both his hands in my hair and pulled my face down to meet his, groaning as I grazed my tongue across his lips and deepened the kiss. I rocked in his lap, my thighs clenching around him.

"Ahem…" I froze, realizing that Piper was still in the room. Austin didn't seem to care, his fingers slipping under my shirt.

I looked over my shoulder at Piper, raising an eyebrow. "Don't stop on my account." he smiled. "You really do change something in the air, just by being close. When you're excited, it's almost as intoxicating as touching you."

I opened my mouth to shoot back a retort, but Austin had managed to slip his hand under my bra and ran his thumb over my nipple, causing me to gasp instead. He did it a second time, sending a jolt of pleasure straight to my core. I whimpered, feeling my panties begin to soak. Austin captured my mouth with his, his tongue exploring me while his hand did the same, kneading my breast and teasing my nipple until it was a hard point.

"They're coming back soon," Piper murmured, his voice sounding husky. He was right, we couldn't just go full carnal on the communal couch. I ran my hand through Austin's hair, gently pulling back from his lips. His hands reluctantly slid from my breasts, back down to my waist, and I could've sworn he was pouting.

"Next time." I smiled at him, and he grinned back, his pupils large and dilated. I shifted off of his lap to sit back on the couch, adjusting my bra. Austin didn't seem to like the sudden distance, and he pulled me over, so I was sitting on his lap instead, his arms wrapping around my waist again.

"I'll be good," he whispered in my ear, and I didn't believe him for a second, but I didn't think he was about to let me go either, so I just relaxed into his arms. Piper had been spot on, and not even a minute later, Cain stalked back into the room with Wyatt in tow. They both stilled as they got close, and I saw Cain's eyes flash with red, like a spark of a flame in the ashes. Cain looked at me, taking in my slightly rumpled appearance, and at Austin, whose face was buried in my hair, and grimaced.

"This is what I mean. It's already getting out of hand," he snapped at Wyatt, sitting down in front of us. Wyatt chose a seat beside Austin and gently tried to untangle his arms from around my waist.

"Austin, Addy has to go home at some point. And you have work, remember?" he told him gently. Austin's arms loosened, and I slipped off his lap carefully, moving to stand by Piper, just out of his reach.

"She can go, but she'll come back, right?" Austin whispered, eyes imploring. Wyatt eyed him wearily, but he behaved and didn't leap off the couch at me or anything.

"I..." I shot a look at Cain, who was glowering at everyone in the room. "I will come back, of course. At least, until I can figure out how to make this..." I held up my hands. "Calm down. I don't want any of you going crazy," I told him.

I yelped when Piper suddenly snaked his hand around my wrist and pulled me down into his lap. "Oh, I believe that ship has sailed, love." He laughed, hands slipping under my shirt to tickle my stomach. I blushed furiously as fresh desire ached between my legs, and Wyatt shot up, pulling me out of Piper's lap and moving me safely out of reach. I noticed his hand stayed on my wrist, so maybe his motives weren't entirely pure either.

"Jesus Christ, Piper, we don't just grab women and fondle them!" Cain barked out. Piper held up his hands in surrender.

"Addy said it was fine, or wait, when do you say that?" he mused, eyes unfocused. "Sorry, maybe you haven't said it yet." Cain groaned, rubbing his hand over his face.

"I'll take you home," Wyatt announced. "Cain can watch these two and make sure they don't jump off the roof or anything stupid." I winced, wishing that wasn't such a genuine concern.

"I can come back after work tomorrow," I told Austin. "But no more sending snakes to my lab. They might eat my research subjects." I smiled, and he grinned and nodded. Piper gave me a little wave as Wyatt quickly ushered me out the basement door.

The fresh air felt good on my face, and it helped me clear my head a little bit. Wyatt was still holding onto my wrist—I wasn't sure he even realized he was doing it anymore. "My apartment's this way," I pointed and led him out of the alley, my heart giving a little tug as we walked away from the studio.

Chapter Eleven

Wyatt

I think Cain had good reason to be worried. He hated change, and most of the time, it was a bit of an overreaction on his part. Piper had told me it took months for Cain to accept he'd be sticking around and then, when Austin found them, it was another couple of months before he was okay with him. It only took a month for Cain to get used to me, but I didn't remember much from back then. I hadn't been in the best state of mind. This was a much bigger change for him than it had been with any of us, though. Cain was worried because Addy offered something we hadn't had before.

Hope.

All of us had accepted the fact that we were going to be alone. I knew I had. Sure, we'd occasionally meet a woman who was interested in a quick hook-up with the freaky guy at the bar. Nobody ever stuck around, though, and they definitely didn't want to be close to us. We didn't have friends outside of our little group but, at least, now we had each other. It had been much lonelier before. Addy was a grenade being lobbed right in the middle of our boring, lonely existence. She was someone who might stick around because, unbelievably, she was just as lonely and isolated as we were. That was what I thought Cain was struggling to understand. Addy looked normal enough, so she couldn't possibly be as sad and as desperate for contact as we were. However, I knew better. I'd felt that ache inside her when I saw her memories. I could see the pain she carried because it was so similar to my own.

If she stayed, though, how would that even work? Austin didn't get possessive about things as we did. Everything was simpler to him. And Piper, well, he wouldn't have a problem with sharing. I knew that from experience. Cain was an enigma, like with most things, and he was still too focused on hating Addy to concern himself with these kinds of questions. As for me... I'd felt a sharp pang of jealousy when I saw her on Austin's lap, her lips swollen and hair a mess. But I also knew my friends needed to have that chance for a connection, too, so if Addy chose Austin, I would be okay with that. Having her near was good enough to keep some of the pain at bay. And maybe, if at some point she wanted something from me, I would happily give it, no strings attached.

Addy walked me to her apartment building, which really was close by, only two blocks from our studio. She didn't complain that I was still holding onto her, and the simple touch made my skin feel like it could light up the evening. She fished her keys out of her bag as we neared the door, but stopped just short of the entrance. I followed her gaze and saw that the front door was broken; the glass busted in the window like someone had tried to get inside.

"Was it like that this morning?" I asked and moved ahead of her to pull at the door. It opened, and the latch unlocked from the inside.

"No," she breathed, clutching her keys tightly. "This is new." We both looked around. It was a relatively pleasant neighborhood, mainly students and campus staff members. Sure, we had the occasional crimes of opportunity and, sometimes, the frats would get rowdy and get into some shit, but otherwise, break-ins weren't really the norm.

"Come on, let's get inside," I murmured and held the door open for her. Addy stepped gingerly over the broken glass in the foyer, and I stayed close behind her as we headed up to her floor.

"It was probably just someone trying to get to the mailboxes," Addy reasoned as we waited for the elevator doors to open. I wanted to agree with her, but weird shit tended to happen around us too often for this to be just an unrelated incident. Sure enough, Addy slowed to a stop in front of me, and I nearly collided with her back. "Oh, come the fuck on," she groaned. We had stopped in front of what I assumed was her apartment.

"You didn't happen to leave it open when you left this morning?" I asked hopefully, but she shook her head. "God damn it..." I pulled the knife I kept on me out of my pocket, flipping it open before I nudged the door with my foot, peering inside. It had been kicked in, and the door frame was splintered from the force. I walked inside slowly, looking around. The place had been trashed. I heard a sharp intake of breath behind me as Addy took in the wreckage.

"Go back outside and call your landlord," I whispered, and she nodded, her eyes filling with tears. I waited until she was back outside before I continued into the apartment, stepping over the debris as carefully as I could. Dishes had been pulled out of the cupboards and smashed across the kitchen counter. A bookshelf was pulled over, and piles of torn-up books were scattered across the living room floor. Her kitchen table was flipped on its side, the chairs around it smashed to pieces, and anything with a cushion had been slashed to ribbons with some kind of knife.

Pushing open the nearest door with my foot, I peered inside. The bathroom was wrecked, the sink partially hanging off the wall, like someone had tried to rip it out with their bare hands. The mirror was smashed, and bits of blood and mirror shards littered the floor. When I got to the last door—which I had to assume led to her bedroom—it was fully shut, and I hesitated a moment before quietly turning the handle and cracking it open.

"Oh, fuck me..." I muttered, taking in the wreckage.

The person who had trashed the apartment was lying in Addy's bed, eyes lifeless, as he faced up at the ceiling. He was clutching one of Addy's blouses, tangled up in her bedsheets, his own clothes nowhere to be found. From the looks of it, he'd sliced his own throat with a kitchen knife, which was still lying beside him on the bed.

I backed out of the room quickly and slammed the door, shoving my knife in my pocket. Addy walked back in, still holding her phone, her eyes wide with fear. "What's wrong?" she asked.

"You need to call the police," I told her quietly, my heart pounding in my chest.

It took the police and EMTs five minutes to arrive, and the landlord appeared shortly after. I stayed with Addy in the hallway while the EMTs went inside to check on the guy in her room. I was pretty sure he was dead, judging by the amount of blood all over everything, but I guess they wanted to be sure. After a little while, they came back out with the stretcher, a black body bag strapped on top. Addy stifled a small sob, and I reflexively put my arm around her.

"Hold on a moment," one officer requested. "Miss, would you mind taking a look at his face to see if you can identify him?" Addy grimaced, but nodded, her mouth set in a thin line. She walked over to the officer, and the closest EMT unzipped the bag, just enough for the guy's head to be visible. Addy looked confused for a split second, then her face went stark white.

"Oh god, it's Pete," Addy told the officer. "Peter, um... McKenzie, I think. He was a researcher on campus. We worked in the same lab together." She backed away from the stretcher, and the EMT quickly closed up the bag, offering her a sympathetic smile before continuing down the hall.

"Were you in a relationship with Peter?" the officer asked, taking notes on a little pad. "Had something happened recently at work that might've upset or angered him?" Addy crossed her arms over her chest, her eyes shining with tears.

"No, nothing, I don't think," she told him earnestly. "I barely knew him. We just exchanged 'hello' sometimes. I don't think I've ever even seen him outside the lab before... uh... this," she trailed off, hands digging into her arms. The officer frowned and nodded, jotting that down.

"So he'd never been here before?" he pressed. "You never told him where you lived?" Addy shook her head, chewing on her lip.

"My address would've been with my personnel file," she offered. "It would be pretty easy to find it if, he'd wanted to." The officer pursed his lips and closed the notebook with a heavy sigh.

"Well, miss, I think you've been very fortunate today. We'll do a bit of digging into Mr. McKenzie's records, but it looks to me like he had an unhealthy fixation on you and couldn't take it anymore." He looked back into the apartment, where several other officers were still taking pictures. "We should be done here in a couple of hours, but I don't think your landlord will be able to fix this door until tomorrow at least, by the looks of it. Do you have somewhere you can stay tonight?" he asked and looked over at me, where I was doing my best to blend into the wall. "Can you stay with your friend there?" He said friend with an edge that made me bristle.

"Of course she can stay with me. Can she grab some of her clothes and stuff, at least?" I asked, standing up straight and moving to Addy's side. The officer hesitated, but then nodded.

"Sure thing, just try not to touch too much," he told her gently, and she nodded, wiping her eyes quickly. I waited outside while he escorted her in, and she came out a few minutes later, holding a duffle bag full of stuff. I took the bag out of her hands and slung it over my shoulder. With my hand on her back, I guided her gently toward the elevators and back outside.

CHAPTER TWELVE

Cain

As soon as Addy left the building, it was as if the air grew stagnant again. The buzzing in my head, which was the constant, unending torture that had plagued me for most of my life, started up as soon as the door closed, and I gritted my teeth. Austin didn't make a break for the door at least, which I'd been half-expecting, but he sat dejected like an abandoned dog, the snakes on his wrists coiling and shifting along his arms restlessly. After a while, he got up and trudged upstairs, and I followed him a moment later, just to make sure he was only going to his room and not trying to sneak out the front door. I waited until I heard the click of his door shutting before traipsing down to the basement, grabbing a cigarette out of my pocket.

When I checked back in on Piper, he was passed out, snoring in the chair. I took a long drag, letting the smoke curl in my lungs, and went back upstairs. Of course, the groceries were still strewn across the floor. I swore under my breath and started to put everything away in the proper places, not that anyone else fucking cared.

The cigarette dropped ash on the floor as I loaded some apples into the fridge. Piper had done a halfway decent job shopping this time. It was honestly a miracle that none of us had gotten scurvy by now. Once everything was put away, I threw the empty bags under the sink and grabbed one of the apples, chewing on it mechanically as I sat down at the kitchen table. The buzzing against my temples increased and, for a horrible moment, it drowned out the world, my vision clouding in a haze of red. When it finally subsided a few minutes later, I gasped in a breath, blinking to get my eyes to clear. There was a charred handprint on the table where my hand had been resting, and the only thing left of the apple was a smoking pile of ash on the floor by my feet.

I scowled and brushed the ash off my jeans as best I could, feeling a headache growing at the base of my skull. The attacks happened randomly, and usually without warning. I'd almost burned the kitchen down once before, so now Wyatt had fire extinguishers stashed in every room of the house. We had no clue why they happened. I just accepted that they were part of the nightmare that was my being. This was why all of this shit with Addy was so dangerous. We were isolated here for a reason. Each one of us was dangerous, either to others, or ourselves, or both. We couldn't just keep inviting in strays to live with us, especially not the ones who made us feel so fucking good. Someone was going to end up hurt, or dead, and then I would be left cleaning up that mess as well.

The door opened on the main floor, and I swore again. Fucking Austin always forgot to lock up after his clients left. I shoved myself up from the table, bracing for the inevitable burst of nausea that usually accompanied the headaches. When nothing happened, I frowned, rubbing my temple, checking to see if my head was still attached to my body. It was, unfortunately, but the headache did seem to have subsided, which was a wonderful and suspicious occurrence. The buzzing settled down, barely a thrum behind my eyes. I groaned in relief, but it morphed into frustration when I saw Wyatt trudge up the stairs, Addy close behind him.

"What the fuck, Wyatt?" I snarled, clenching my hands at my sides. "I thought you were taking her home. She was supposed to stay there." My jaw clenched as Wyatt squared his shoulders and dropped a duffle bag on the floor.

"Plans changed," he replied shortly. "Addy needs to stay here for the night."

"You guys are impossible," I announced, throwing up my hands. "I will take her home then, if you can't manage it." I took a step forward just as Addy stepped out from behind him, her eyes red with tears. She looked a lot smaller than she had when they'd left, as if she'd shrunk somehow after leaving the house.

"Some dude broke into her apartment and slit his throat in her bed." Wyatt grimaced. Oh fuck, well wasn't that just our luck. I sighed and threw up my hands, sitting back down at the table.

"Fine!" I snapped. "Fine, she can take my room. That way, you drug addicts won't end up smothering her in her sleep." I rubbed a hand over my face, fucking exhausted with life. Now I got to sleep on a dirty old sofa. That was just the perfect end to this day.

"I don't need your room," Addy huffed, crossing her arms over her chest. "I'll just sleep in the basement."

"Don't be stupid, you're sleeping in the damn room," I growled at her, feeling the faint hold I had on my temper starting to fray. "I can't be worrying about you, wandering around the studio during the night." That comment earned me a withering glare.

"What, do you think I'm going to trash the place?" Addy exclaimed, casting a glance around the kitchen. "I think that's already been taken care of, don't you?" She had a hard edge to her voice that hadn't been there before they'd left. Clearly, she was pretty worked up over the dead guy in her apartment.

"Why don't you stay in a fancy hotel if our home isn't fucking good enough for you?" I yelled. Rage flashed in her eyes, and she looked like she wanted to hit me. She stepped over her bag, her hands balled into fists.

"I never asked to come here!" Addy yelled back. I saw Wyatt sidestep out of the room, disappearing upstairs before things turned violent. Coward.

"Then maybe next time keep your fucking hands to yourself so nobody offs themselves in your bed," I snarled. That seemed to do it. I watched with a twisted sense of satisfaction as her temper spilled over. Addy shoved me in the chest, and I fell back a step, smirking as visceral rage flashed in her eyes. She swung her fist at me, and I caught it, trapping her hand in mine.

My mind quieted when I touched her skin, the pressure that normally pushed against my skull fading out into blissful calm. Oblivious to her effects on me, Addy yelled in frustration and swung at me with her other fist. I caught that one easily as well. She struggled to free her hands, cursing me and kicking at me viciously. I kept a firm grip on her, dodging the kicks as I propelled her back until she bumped against the fridge. I pinned her hands above her head, looming over her while she struggled.

"Let me go!" Addy shrieked, her eyes blazing with a fiery rage that threatened to scorch me from the inside out.

"You've got quite the fucking temper, don't you?" I remarked, earning another glare. "I will let you go once you calm down and behave," I told her evenly, trying to ignore the shot of pleasure running through me when she snarled, aiming a kick at my thigh. Moving swiftly, I used my legs to pin hers against the fridge, pressing flush against her.

"Quit trying to hurt me, and I'll let you go." I smirked down at her. I watched Addy's chest rising and falling with each shaky breath, her face tilted up to meet my stare with a glare of her own. No wonder the guys were losing their minds over her.

She was gorgeous even when she was furious—especially when she was furious.

My head was spinning, being this close, with her hips pushing up against me. Heat curled in my hands, and I saw her face flush with the sudden warmth. Her lips parted with the smallest gasp, and I moved my face closer to hers, letting a little more of the heat lick at her skin. She narrowed her eyes at me, wriggling her hips against mine.

"You said you would let me go," Addy murmured, her body tensing and arching against me. I clenched my jaw as my body responded to hers, and she smirked.

"Are you going to behave?" I growled back, sending another lick of heat through my hands, making her gasp. As an answer, she captured my mouth with hers. Her kiss was like an electric shock, jolting every nerve in my body. I groaned when she sucked on my bottom lip and hissed when she bit it.

She drew back with an impish grin, and I licked at the blood welling up on my lip. She was a twisted little minx, and my dick was painfully hard, pressing against the fly of my jeans.

"I guess that's a no," I murmured. Shifting, I moved her hands up above her head, and grabbed both her wrists in one hand, freeing up my other one. I slid my finger down her jaw, almost hot enough to hurt. She hissed out a breath between her teeth as I trailed it down the side of her neck.

"There's a lot I can do with this," I whispered in her ear, and she shivered as I slid my finger down her chest and across her stomach. I undid the button of her jeans and slipped my hand inside, and she let out a shuddered moan when my fingers brushed against the damp fabric of her panties. I circled her clit through the thin material, sending another quick rush of heat through my finger. She moaned louder and bucked into my hand, the noise making my dick throb.

"How long has it been since someone touched you?" I asked, feeling her desire against my fingers. Addy whimpered, arching as I pressed against her clit again with another stroke of heat. I leaned down to capture her mouth, letting her taste the blood she'd drawn from my lip. I toyed with her clit mercilessly until she moaned into my mouth, writhing against me as she came and soaked my fingers with her juices.

I finally released her wrists, and she brought her hands down to rest on my chest. Her eyes were softer now, her rage apparently forgotten for the time being. Her face was still flushed, lips swollen and stained red from my bloody lip. My head was spinning, like I'd had too much to drink. I pushed away from her abruptly, freeing her from where I'd trapped her against the fridge. "Put your bag in my room down the hall," I ordered, pointing down the hall. "You'll sleep in there for tonight." Before she could protest, I stepped over her things and headed downstairs to clear my head.

She was going to be trouble. I just knew it.

CHAPTER THIRTEEN

Addison

I didn't know if I could take much more craziness in my life. On top of everything else, I mourned for my apartment, the safe haven that I'd lived in since I started my master's thesis two years ago. I didn't have much in the way of earthly possessions, but the ones I had meant a lot, and I'd packed up as many of the undamaged ones as I could to try to preserve at least some piece of my home. I didn't think I could go back there now, not after what Pete had done.

Poor, sad Pete. Why the fuck did he have to do that on my bed? I sat in Cain's room, my bag at my feet, trying to figure out what to do next. I'd called the faculty head and let her know about Pete because there would probably be some kind of process to sort out with his project and the grant money he'd no longer be using. She let me know how sorry she was and told me to take the week off to recover. I thanked her and hung up, falling back on the bed with a sigh.

And what the fuck was up with Cain? I could still feel the ghost of his hand around my wrists. He ran so hot and cold that I couldn't keep up with him from one moment to the next. Did he hate me? Was it just my weird, addictive skin that had made him touch me like that? How would I even begin to sort that out? Ugh. I pushed the heels of my palms against my eyes, which were sore and puffy from crying. I grabbed for my bag, digging through the mess of stuff I'd shoved inside while the police officer had been standing next to me. He hadn't even been decent enough to turn away when I'd gone through my underwear drawer, the fucking perv. Cain's room had an on-suite bathroom, which was convenient. I needed to clean off after the day I'd had, and I felt grimy after walking through my desecrated apartment.

The shower helped somewhat, the cool water soothing my swollen eyes and washing off some of the horrors of the day. I was feeling moderately better by the time I was done, and I threw on an oversized shirt that I'd turned into a nightgown years ago. The fabric was fading and thin, rubbed soft after hundreds of rounds in the laundry, and it was my favourite thing to sleep in.

I curled up in Cain's bed, listening to the sounds of an unfamiliar home as I tried to drift off to sleep. The bed smelled like campfire and bitter spice, just like he did. Sleep found me more easily than I'd anticipated, considering all that I'd seen today.

Something woke me up sometime in the early morning, and I felt the bed shift slightly beside me. I was vaguely aware of someone's breath on my neck and an arm snaking over my waist. It must've been Austin. He was quiet after that. A steady warmth pressed against my back. I drifted back to sleep, listening to him breathe in the darkness.

When I woke again, the sun was shining through a crack in the blinds, and I was alone in the bed. Rolling over to look around blearily, I wondered if I'd just imagined my late-night visitor. I knew the boys didn't exist on a normal sleep schedule, so I didn't bother getting dressed before I wandered out to the kitchen in search of coffee. There had been a coffeemaker sitting on the counter yesterday, but whether or not it was actually usable was another thing altogether. I started to hunt through the cupboards, looking for coffee grounds or filters. A check of the bottom cupboards produced nothing, so I started on the higher cabinets. A bunch of bachelors living together left a lot to be desired. Their kitchen was in a woeful state of neglect.

I spied a coffee can in the second to last cabinet I checked, but of course, because everyone who lived here was a fucking giant, it was out of reach. I stood up on my tiptoes, reaching as high as I could, and managed to just poke the damn can further back on the shelf. "Damn you," I muttered, pushing against the counter as if that would help me grow the extra four inches I needed.

Hands slipped around my hips, tracing along the waistband of my panties. It seemed that my night-shirt had ridden up a little high during my struggles. I yelped in surprise, sliding back off the counter. The hands steadied me, and I saw a familiar-looking set of bracelets out of the corner of my eye. I hadn't been expecting anyone up this early, least of all Piper.

"Good morning, little spider," he murmured, hands moving up under my shirt to tickle my stomach.

I squirmed as he hit a ticklish spot on my side. "Good morning," I replied softly, and he pressed a kiss against my shoulder.

"I had a dream about you last night," Piper told me, hands drawing little patterns along my ribs. "I was dying, all alone in the desert, and then I found you, my little spider, just lying out in the sand." His fingers slid up over my breasts, rolling my nipples until I pressed back against him with a quiet moan. "I was starving, so I devoured you," he murmured, spinning me so my back was against the counter. "You tasted so good, like honey and peach nectar." Piper knelt down in front of me, sliding my panties down my legs and discarding them on the floor. "I gorged myself until I burst."

He lifted my ankle up and hooked it over his shoulder, then shifted up so fast I nearly toppled backward onto the counter. I caught myself on my elbows, but before I could scold him, his mouth was on me, licking up the length of my slit. He grabbed my hips to hold me still and plunged his tongue inside me, and I threw back my head as pleasure rushed into my core. I tangled my hand in his hair, my hips rocking against his face as he fucked me with his tongue. I couldn't hold back a guttural moan as he ravished me with his mouth, shifting up to focus on my swollen clit. He was devouring me just as he had in his dream, and I bucked my hips as he took my clit between his lips and sucked, the pressure building like a tidal wave inside me. I noticed movement in my periphery and looked over to see Wyatt standing shirtless by the stairs, hair mussed from sleep. I felt the blush spread across my cheeks at being caught in such a compromising position. Just then, Piper lashed at my sensitive nub with his tongue, and the wave of pressure crested. I forgot that Wyatt was watching, and I cried out, gripping Piper's hair as I climaxed. Piper continued to devour me, lapping at my slit until my legs were trembling and I could barely hold myself up anymore.

He finally released me, sitting me up on the counter because, I was pretty sure, I would've collapsed otherwise. He kissed me deeply so I could taste myself on his tongue and gave me a roguish smile. "Thanks for breakfast, love," he told me and nodded to Wyatt as he passed, heading downstairs to do god knows what.

I was breathless, still shivering from the orgasm Piper had given me, and embarrassed that Wyatt had witnessed all of it. He didn't seem particularly fazed, but it was always hard to tell with those damn sunglasses he had on. He walked up to the counter where I was sitting and moved between my legs. My breath caught in my throat as he leaned close... and reached up above my head to snatch the coffee can I'd been trying to grab earlier. He gave me a little smirk, like he knew exactly what he'd done. "Interested in some coffee, or did Piper's mouth do the trick?" he asked dryly, and I gave him a playful shove on the shoulder. Shit, he was muscular. It was like slapping a boulder.

"Coffee would be great, thanks," I told him, and he grinned at me. Much to my complete embarrassment, he bent down to scoop my discarded panties off the floor, twirling them around his finger as he walked to the coffee machine.

"You know, it's pretty risky to walk around here pants-less," he said with a cheeky smirk, and I shot him a dirty look. He set about making the coffee, the thin purple fabric still clutched in his hand. Once he had the coffee going, he sat down at the table and held them up again as if they were the most fascinating thing in the world. I rolled my eyes and hopped off the counter, now fairly certain I wouldn't melt into a puddle. I held out my hand impatiently.

"Finder's keepers," Wyatt replied. I tried to snatch them out of his hands, but he was too quick, holding them out of my reach.

"Oh, come on!" I laughed, reaching over him to grab for them. He took that opportunity to snatch me, pulling me into his lap. "You guys are like cats with catnip, I swear," I huffed, as he gave me a gentle squeeze, nuzzling his face into my neck.

"We're just so damn lonely," he murmured. "And then you drop in, all irresistible. It's like torture, not getting to touch you." My face must've been burning scarlet by that point. Never in my life had anyone described me in that way, and the attention they were focusing on me was a heady cocktail I could easily get drunk on. I traced my finger along Wyatt's tattoo, following the swirls down his left bicep and along his forearm.

"Did you do these yourself?" I asked, shifting in his lap so I could face him.

"Yeah, not all at once, but over the years I added to it," Wyatt replied, his hand drawing patterns along my thigh. "I had another artist do my back, since I couldn't reach there." I'd never seen someone get a tattoo before, but I knew the gist of it: needles and ink. To cover his whole torso must've taken months.

"Does it hurt?" I asked, my fingers drifting down to the dark lines across his ribs.

"It depends on where it is. Some areas have more nerves or thinner skin." He squeezed my thigh. "The pain never bothered me, though," he whispered. "It can even feel good sometimes." I shivered as a trickle of desire ran down my spine. I kissed him softly, just a light brush of my lips against his. He let out a shuddered breath, as if he was barely holding himself together.

The coffee machine dinged, jolting us out of the daze we'd slipped into, and he laughed at the timing. I slipped out of his arms, pulling my night shirt down to cover myself. I definitely needed to wear pants in this house. Several layers of clothing probably would be best. He followed me, grabbed two mugs out of a different cabinet, and poured me a cup of coffee.

"I've got a client coming in this afternoon for a sleeve," Wyatt told me. "Afterwards, maybe I can show you a bit of how I work." He smiled darkly, and I shivered again. "Come to the studio rooms around 11 p.m.," he instructed. I watched him stick my panties in his pocket, and he smirked before heading downstairs.

If this was going to be a habit for him, I was going to have to go shopping.

Chapter Fourteen

Austin

The house felt different, even my little friends sensed it. All around my room, I could see flashes of scales as their bodies moved, unusually restless this early in the day. I sat by the window, looking out through the crack I'd opened to breathe in the day, and my twin vipers twined up one of my legs, jostling and hissing as they fought for space. Over on my bed, my sheets moved like they were possessed, the space claimed by more of my friends during my absence last night.

I had smelled Addy in the air from the moment she'd arrived, but I wanted to prove that I could be good, so I stayed in my room. It was nice to listen to the house adjust to Addy. I heard the floor creak under her feet and the walls hum as her breath filled the rooms with new life. I overheard Wyatt tell Piper that Addy couldn't go home yet because someone had broken in and died in her bed. My lips curled in disgust at the thought of someone coming into my den—*room, it's a room*—and fouling it with their presence. Addy could have stayed in my room if she wanted, my friends would keep her safe and warm. Nobody could come in here without my permission. I would stay up all night to make sure.

Cain's door opened and closed, and the floor creaked its new Addy sounds. That made sense. Cain knew that if she stayed there, no one would hurt her, because no one could hurt Cain. Cain was the leader, so he made the rules, although Wyatt didn't like when I said that. Wyatt made rules too sometimes, but he was smart, so that was okay. That's what Cain had said. Piper tried to make rules, but Cain and Wyatt both warned me to ask them first before listening to him. Piper got time mixed up sometimes, so he'd say things that didn't work today but would work next week. It was okay though, because Piper always forgot his rules anyway, so he didn't care if I listened or not.

I waited patiently until the house told me Addy was asleep, Wyatt was asleep, and Piper was doing something on the floor that sounded like crying, but I couldn't be sure. I didn't hear noises for Cain, but he could move like smoke if he wanted to, so the house sometimes couldn't tell me where he was. Creeping down the stairs cautiously, I found the kitchen empty. I flicked my lip ring with my tongue. Addy's scent was so strong in the kitchen, it made my knees weak.

The floor creaked its Austin sounds as I walked up to Cain's door. Normally, I would never come here, because Cain didn't like people in his room, but I thought it might be different since Addy was already there. I slipped inside and, for a moment, I just watched her sleep, curled up on her side with her dark hair fanned out on the pillow. I was still proving that I could be good so that she would stay, so I didn't wake her up, but I couldn't resist climbing up on the bed and curling up against her, nestling my face against her shoulder. She smelled a little like Cain now, and I thought about all the ways I could make her smell like me, and it excited me. I had to behave though, so she wouldn't leave, so I stayed perfectly still and listened to her sleep.

I must've dozed off for a while, but my eyes flew open when I heard the door creak, my body tensing around Addy protectively. I saw Cain standing in the doorway, eyes flashing red like the cigarettes he smokes, and I knew I was in trouble. Careful to not disturb Addy, I slipped my arm off her waist and slunk over to the door. Cain grabbed my arm and hauled me out into the hallway, swinging the door shut behind him.

"We do not sneak into Addy's bed," he told me in a low voice. "You always wait for permission, and you give her space when she wants it. Do you understand?" I nodded, chewing on my lip ring. "We can at least pretend to be civilized human beings and not attack her like feral cats while she's here."

I glowered at him. I wasn't some mangey tom cat like the ones I heard fighting in the alley. If she let me, I would make her safe and warm and happy, just like she made me feel when she touched me. "Alright," I hissed at him, and he kept staring until I dropped my eyes to the floor.

"Wyatt has a client tomorrow, so he asked me to take Addy back to her apartment and see if it's safe for her to go in yet. Why don't you come with us? It's been a while since you've gone outside," he suggested, and I clenched my fists. Cain always wanted me to go outside, but it was perfectly nice inside. People were outside, and I didn't like people. "I bet Addy would feel safer if you came with us," Cain continued, and I perked up. I could keep her safe and show her I could be good, prove that I could protect her.

"Okay, I'll come," I whispered, and Cain smirked like he had known I'd agree to it all along. He was blocking the bedroom door, making sure I wouldn't try to sneak in again, I guess.

I went back up to my room and stayed there, dozing on the chair by the window as I listened to the street wake up for the day. Piper got up early today, which was unusual for him, especially on the nights he made a lot of noises. Cain's door opened and closed too, and the floor creaked Addy's steps into the kitchen. Cain hadn't told me when we would go outside today, but I wanted to be ready, just in case. I shook a ball python out of a pair of jeans onto the floor. They smelled okay, but they had a hole in the knce. Hopefully, that was okay for Addy. I found a shirt which might've been Wyatt's in my closet, and it only had one stain on it and no holes, so it would work to go outside today. I didn't know what to do, if I should go downstairs to wait by the door, or if I should stay here until Cain said it was time to go. The ball python tried to climb up my pant leg, but I shooed him back, over to the closet. Cain said I shouldn't bring my friends with me on outside days, because people didn't like to see snakes in the city. I argued that people didn't like to see me in the city either, but he still made me go outside, anyway.

The kitchen told me it had a lot of visitors today, and Addy's scent mixed with Piper and Wyatt and coffee, and I bounced on my toes, waiting to go. I finally heard Cain's sounds on the stairs and burst out of my room, bounding down the stairs three steps at a time to the kitchen. It smelled so good in the kitchen, I started to salivate, even with the coffee mingling in which I had never understood the appeal of. I found some lunch meat in the fridge that hadn't gone green yet and ate some to fill my stomach. Another Cain rule was that we eat human foods in the house. I think that was because he caught me eating a mouse once, and it made him sick.

"Morning Austin!" I yanked my head out of the fridge and beamed. Addy had put all of her hair up on top of her head today, leaving her neck tantalizingly bare. She wasn't wearing one of her fancy shirts this time, just a regular tee shirt like mine, only without a stain. Addy was so normal-looking. I bet no one glared or yelled at her when she walked around outside.

I slammed the fridge closed and ran up to Addy, wrapping my arms around her tightly and lifting her up off her feet. She gave a small cry of surprise, but I felt her hug me back, and my heart swelled with joy. I pressed my nose against a spot behind her ear and tried my best not to bite her. My teeth ached with the effort. "Austin? I can't breathe." Addy gasped. Oops—I loosened my hold, and she slipped back down to the ground, taking a deep breath.

"Sorry," I rasped with an apologetic smile. Addy patted my cheek, clearly not mad about being squished, and I watched her pour herself some more coffee from the machine on the counter. I wrinkled my nose. "Why do you like that?" I asked her, following her to the table and sitting across from her. I kept my hands to myself to show her I could. Wyatt told me he liked coffee because it helped him stay awake. I tried it once, it tasted like dirt and made my chest hurt a lot.

Addy shrugged and took a sip. "I like the taste and the smell, too, I guess. It helps me wake up in the morning. It warms me up and helps me prepare for the day." I huffed and wriggled in my chair. I could warm her up better in the morning. She didn't need coffee for that. It appeared she did like the taste of it somehow, because she kept sipping it and looked very content. Maybe Wyatt made terrible coffee, and it was supposed to taste better than dirt. I waited until she took another sip and shifted out of my chair to kiss her, swiping her lips with my tongue. Her lips parted in surprise, and I explored her mouth, tasting the bitter coffee on her tongue. The coffee was still the same, but it tasted sweeter when it mingled with Addy.

I pulled back and shook my head, Addy's eyes wide with shock. "I don't understand coffee," I whispered sadly. She laughed like I had made a joke, and I smiled to see her happy. The stairs groaned with Cain's arrival as he came stalking up from the main floor.

"Ready to go?" he asked Addy sharply, and she gave him an irritated look, which he ignored. Cain hated everyone at first, but he'd stop being mean eventually when he forgot that he hated her.

"Sure, I'll just grab my jacket and my purse," Addy replied and set her mug in the sink before heading back into Cain's room. He gave me a once-over, and I shifted to hide the stain on my shirt. He always told me to do laundry more, but I kept forgetting, and I didn't like the smell of the soap, anyway.

When Addy returned, I sprang to my feet, sad that her arms were covered up now. Cain grunted and walked back down to the main floor, leaving us to follow behind. I shook my arms and legs at the door, making sure none of my friends had gotten tucked away somewhere. Hopping down the front steps, I hurried to catch up to Addy and Cain, bristling as the outside smells hit me all at once. I hooked my arm around Addy's shoulders, and the outside didn't feel so bad with her hip bumping against mine. She smiled and leaned into me, and my chest puffed out with pride.

Addy's home was in a building not very far from ours, and she pointed out the places she liked to visit as we walked. According to her, they made wonderful coffee and pastries at a little café across from our studio, but I'd take her word for it. There's no way I'd spend ten dollars on bitter dirt water. I noticed people reacted to Addy differently than they did to my friends when she walked past them on the sidewalk. Their eyes would meet hers, and they would give her a friendly smile or a polite nod. A lot of the men would also give her a quick once over, much to my irritation. Eventually, their eyes would shift to me, and their smiles would drop. Some people looked angry, like I was insulting them with how I looked. Other people just looked scared or concerned. I hunched my shoulders and stared down at the sidewalk, letting Addy lead the way.

There was a sizeable piece of plywood over the entrance to Addy's building, so I guess they hadn't gotten around to fixing it yet. Her apartment still had police tape all over the door, and Cain and I waited while she spoke to someone on the phone about it. She started getting pretty angry and, by the time she hung up the phone, her face was red and her eyes were shining, the whole hallway smelling like her rage.

"They can't close it as a crime scene until they finish processing the body, and there's some hold-up at the lab," she told us, pinching the bridge of her nose. "I can't even go inside to get any more of my things, and my landlord said it could be a week before my door gets fixed. Fuck!" she exclaimed, kicking the wall in frustration. Cain looked a little amused by the outburst and just shrugged.

"Whatever. Do you have enough shit to get you through the week?" he asked. Addy bit her lip, and I saw her mind working quickly.

"I guess so, but I don't want to put you out of your room for another night, let alone a week." She sighed. I immediately opened my mouth to offer my room, but Cain stopped me with a look.

"Don't worry about it. We'll sort it out. Let's just get back then," he muttered and shoved his hands in his pockets, fishing for a cigarette, as we headed back toward the elevators.

The walk back to the studio was a lot quieter. Addy didn't seem to want to talk much anymore, and Cain had walked up ahead, smoking by himself. Addy looked so sad now, so I put my arm around her shoulders and kissed the side of her head, trying to cheer her up.

"You alright, baby?" A group of guys slowed as they neared us, heading in the opposite direction. Addy stiffened in my arms but ignored them, staring straight ahead. "Come on, give us a smile, then." I scowled at him. Clearly, she wasn't in the mood to smile, or she would. I followed Addy's lead and ignored them.

"Ditch the freak show, I know how to make you smile," his friend jeered, and he grabbed Addy's arm as we went to pass them. She jerked her arm away from him, and I moved to get between them, staring him down, my teeth flashing.

"Don't fucking touch me, asshole!" Addy snapped, and I put my hand up when he tried to move toward her again. He looked me up and down and sneered, giving me a shove in the chest. I didn't move, didn't react, because Cain told me not to fight anyone, but I wouldn't let them touch Addy again.

"Come on sweetheart, hop off E.T.'s dick and come back to Earth where the real men are," his friend called out, and the guy shoved me again, harder this time. "What, only speak Klingon?" He smirked at me.

"Walk away, asshole, she's not interested," I rasped, my fists clenched at my sides. The guy laughed, turning to his friends. Then he whipped back around, sucker-punching me in the face. I staggered back, tasting blood where I must've bitten my tongue. I wanted to hurt him, make him bleed, rip out his throat, and pour venom into the gaping wound as he writhed on the ground. No fighting though, I had promised. So I stood up straight, holding my ground. Blood dripped down my face as I stared at him, unblinking. This seemed to confuse him, and he looked back at his friends, who were also plainly waiting for me to attack or do something other than glare at them.

Unfortunately for them, Cain stormed up, having noticed the commotion behind him. "Get the fuck out of here," he snarled at them. The one guy turned to say something nasty, but something about Cain's face had him turning white, and they sprinted off down the street. Addy was grabbing my arm, her hand touching my face. I winced when she touched a tender spot on my cheek, and her fingers drew back. I wiped my hand under my nose, and it came back bloody, and more was dripping down onto my shirt. Aw man, it was really stained now.

Addy ran into the café she'd shown me earlier and got a bunch of their napkins. I pressed a handful to my face to try to stop the bleeding while she guided me back to our home. "I can't believe those fuckers!" she exclaimed as we walked inside. "He just attacked you out of nowhere!" Cain wasn't saying much, and I worried that he was mad. I did what he'd asked. I didn't fight them, even though I had wanted to so badly.

"It happens a lot," I whispered, looking down at my feet, and more blood poured out of my nose. Addy led me to Cain's room and into his bathroom, pushing me backward until I sat down on the toilet lid. She took the wad of bloody napkins out of my hand and tossed them in the trash, grabbing a washcloth instead and wetting it before pressing it back under my nose.

"I'll check and see if there's any ice," Addy told me, heading back into the kitchen. Cain stayed behind, leaning against the doorframe. I stared at my feet, waiting for him to start yelling.

"I'm sorry," I told him hoarsely. "I didn't do anything, I swear." He just chuckled quietly.

"I know you didn't do anything, and I don't get why," Cain told me. "Were you worried about upsetting Addy or something?" I looked up at him, confused. Would she have been mad if I had hit them? I thought she would be mad that I didn't defend her better from them, that I let him grab her and didn't rip his arm off.

"You said no fighting. So I didn't fight," I rasped, hunching my shoulders. Cain groaned and rubbed his face.

"Don't start fights." He sighed. "If someone fucking attacks you, you can fucking hit them back." He shook his head. "It's good you didn't though, I guess. We don't need some asshole student filing a complaint against you." He ran a hand through his hair. "Alright... I need to go find a fucking bed, or something. I don't know." He threw up his hands, grumbling as he stalked out of the room. I kept the washcloth pressed to my face, staring at the floor.

Addy came bustling back in holding a little bottle. "No ice, but I got some peroxide to get the blood out of your shirt. Give it here." She held out her hand expectantly. I pulled the shirt over my head, trying not to brush it against my nose. She stuck it in the sink and poured the peroxide over it, rubbing at the stains. She left it soaking in the sink and turned to me next, taking the cloth out of my hand and checking my face. "He didn't do much damage, at least." She pursed her lips, wiping the blood off of my nose and chin as gently as she could. I closed my eyes as her hand cupped my chin, wiping some errant blood smears off my neck. Her kindness made my eyes sting. It felt like someone had taken a piece out of my chest and rubbed salt into it.

I don't ever remember someone caring for me like this. I was sure someone did, at some point. Human babies didn't survive long without a caregiver of some kind. But as far back as my memories went, there was no one. I've been on my own for a very long time.

"I'm sorry he hit you," she murmured, her hand grazing my cheek. My face pressed into her hand, my body responding to her touch like flowers following the sun.

"People like to hurt me," I rasped, shrugging my shoulders. Her face fell, and I looked down, embarrassed. Wyatt and Cain also looked weird, but Wyatt hid it behind his glasses, and Cain was too scary for people to bother. I was weird, but not scary enough to deter them. I figured my face was clean enough now, so I stood and moved past Addy, wanting to just be alone in my room for a while.

Addy grabbed my hand gently, stopping me, and reluctantly I turned back toward her. "Thank you for protecting me," she breathed, touching my chest. "And I'm glad you didn't hit him back. I'd hate to see you get in trouble because of me." She smiled, and my heart lifted.

"I would though," I told her earnestly. "I would've ripped him in half for you." That made her laugh, and I put my arms around her, loving how she felt against my skin. Her fingers trailed along my chest, and she touched one of the small patches of scales that poked through my skin.

"It's funny. At first, I thought these were tattoos," she mused, and I huffed a laugh. She tilted her head up and kissed my cheek, and I smiled despite the ache in my chest.

Addy didn't try to stop me again, and I slipped out of Cain's room and back upstairs, closing my door and locking it. My friends started to stir, hissing as they tasted my pain and fear in the air. When I sat down on the bed, they joined me, wrapping around my arms and slithering over my legs. I was safe in here with them; they told me. At least, I was safe in here.

Chapter Fifteen

Wyatt

I locked the deadbolt on the front door and closed my eyes for a moment, taking a slow breath in. This session tonight had been a marathon. The client was eager to have their sleeve finished, and my shoulders were cramped from sitting hunched over them for six hours. I opened my eyes again reluctantly and went back to clean the room and put away my tools. They'd been very happy with the results at least, and I'd gotten a $100 bonus for getting it done so fast. My clients liked me, and I got a lot of word-of-mouth business because of it. After I'd wiped down the chair, I grabbed the beer I'd stashed in the cupboard and cracked it open, not caring that it was warm at this point. My nerves were so keyed up from the session that my skin burned. Even the lukewarm beer didn't help to tamp down the flames.

A knock on the door made me pause, and I opened it, expecting Cain, but it was Addy. My heart skipped a beat as I took in her presence. I'd invited her, of course, but I wouldn't have been mad if she'd bailed. We'd just been flirting. She gave me a hesitant smile. "You wanted to show me your work?" she reminded me, and I hastened to let her inside.

"Sorry, of course," I replied. "Long day, my brain's a little... yeah." I ran a hand through my hair and closed the door behind her. Addy sat down in the tattoo chair, looking around the room. Just her proximity was enough to calm the itch of need under my skin. When she'd left this afternoon, I'd felt it return, and it had been hard to concentrate on work until they'd returned to the studio. Now that she was in the room, her body so close to mine, I craved the high she gave me.

Her cheeks turned pink, and I realized I'd just been staring at her silently for a little too long now. "Sorry." I shook my head. "It was a big session. They knock a few things loose up here sometimes." I tapped my head, and she laughed.

"What was it today?" Addy asked. I sat on my stool and rolled up beside her so our heads could be level.

"I did a right arm sleeve," I explained, using her arm to demonstrate. "She wanted old-style roses, with climbing vines from her elbow up to her shoulder." My finger brushed against her bare arm as I recreated the pattern against her skin. "Then on her forearm, it was like a forest of thorns, with eyes peering out from the darkness. Eyes are tricky to get right," I told her. "And then she'd wanted another red rose on her wrist here," I picked up her hand, turning it and exposing the tender skin of her wrist. "This is a very painful spot. The skin is so thin here." I traced one of her veins, my own wrist burning.

"How did she handle it?" Addy asked, eyebrows raised. I gave her a coy smile.

"That's why my clients like me so much," I told her, fingers still running along her wrist. "I'm the only artist who can make tattoos painless, even the notoriously bad spots."

Addy frowned slightly. "So you take their pain away? Like you did with my ankle?" she asked, and I nodded. "So where does the pain go, then?"

As an answer, I pulled off my hoodie, which I wore during most of my sessions, and tossed it aside. I just had one of my black tank tops on, my arms exposed, and I turned so she could see the inflamed red lines on my right arm, the ghost of the tattoo I'd done today. She grabbed my hand, looking at the puffy skin on my wrist, the barest shape of a rose still visible.

"God, that looks so painful," she murmured. "Why do you do it?" Her finger hovered over the lines, not quite touching, probably worried about hurting me further. The thought made me smile.

"I like to think I'm helping them," I replied with a shrug. "If I can take away the worst parts of the experience and leave the enjoyment of the tattoo, why not? I'm built to handle the pain." Addy's face told me that this made her sad, and that's not what I wanted to do at all. "It's really okay," I told her quickly. "The pain doesn't last as long as it would for them, and sometimes I can send some of it back out if I need to," I told her. That was a fun trick I'd used a few times when pricks had started fights with me. Nothing sucks more than being punched with the pain of your own hit.

"Here, watch," I told her and took her wrist again. I traced a tiny line, just a little, because I didn't want to actually hurt her, and pushed a little of the pain out. Addy jumped, and her eyes widened as a little strip of red appeared where my finger had been. I ran my finger across it again, pulling the pain back in, and I felt my groin ache from the sharp jolt it gave me. I smiled and pushed the little jolt of pleasure out to Addy, replacing the sting I'd given her. She gave a sharp intake of breath and looked at me with narrowed eyes, her pupils dilating from the rush of pleasure.

"I can do it with other things besides pain." I smirked. "I can give and take a lot of things." To prove my point, I gave her arm a little pinch and pulled the pain quickly, giving back the pleasure in its place. Addy's cheeks flushed, and her lips parted in surprise.

"So you... you enjoy the pain sometimes?" Addy asked, her hand brushing over the tender skin of my arm. I hissed as the nerves pulsed, and I felt my dick jump, growing stiff in my jeans. I sent another sliver of pleasure through her fingers, and she gasped.

"Sometimes. I don't enjoy fights, like when someone is kicking the shit out of me." I laughed, and she rolled her eyes at me, smiling. "But things like the quick sting of the needle from the tattoo gun, that kind of pain can be good," I murmured. "When pain is drawn out slowly and deliberately, it can turn into something better." I leaned over and cupped her cheek, pulling her face toward mine. I kissed her tenderly, and she shifted in the chair to get closer. Her lips parted, and I took that as an invitation to deepen the kiss, my tongue twining with hers as I explored her mouth. I pulled back after a minute, drunk with the feel of her and aching after a day of torturous pleasure with no release, and my control was hanging on by a thread.

"Do you think you'd ever get a tattoo?" I asked her, trying to ease some of the tension building in the tiny room. Addy was still turned toward me, her body terribly inviting, stretched out in my chair. She seemed to think about it for a moment.

"I'd never considered one before, because I didn't want to hurt someone accidentally," she mused. "But I think maybe now I would, if you were the one to do it." She smiled, and I suppressed a groan. God, I would cover her in ink if I could. I'd hold her for hours in this chair until she was trembling and dripping wet from the pleasure of it.

"Of course, I would," I told her hoarsely. "Whatever you want, just name it." Addy smiled at me and leaned back in the chair.

"Where do you think I should get one?" she asked, her eyes dancing in the light. My dick was pressing against the fly of my jeans. I stood up, the pressure from sitting becoming too unbearable. I looked over at her, considering, and tugged her shirt up, exposing her stomach and her ribs.

"Some people like a tattoo here," I murmured, running my finger across her ribs, just underneath her breast. "It's easy to hide under clothes. Rib tattoos are painful, though." I breathed, letting a tiny sliver of pain slide through as I etched across her skin. Addy arched against my finger, hissing, and I replaced the pain immediately, making her hum with pleasure. A little raised line remained, the ghost of the tattoo that didn't exist. I'd written my name, Wyatt, since rib tattoos seemed to often be names. Addy noticed it and smirked at me, cocking an eyebrow.

"You want me to get your name as my first tattoo?" she asked coyly, and I laughed and shook my head. I lifted her shirt up further, and she raised her arms to help me slide it off.

"No, not for your first," I replied, my voice husky as I stared at her body, all the fresh, un-inked skin just begging for my attention. "Maybe after I've covered you in ink, I can sign you like a work of art." I set my knees on either side of her legs, climbing onto the chair so I could get closer to her. Addy settled back into the chair, her hands coming up to rest on my hips as I hovered over her. I unhooked the front clasp of her bra, letting it fall open as my eyes roved over her chest. I pressed my finger along her collarbone, her skin raising up obediently in the outline of a flower. Her eyes closed as she inhaled sharply, and I pushed out another shot of desire until her face softened.

Fuck, she was too tempting. It was sweet, delicious torture. I rolled one of her breasts in my hand, toying with her nipple until it hardened. I pinched it between my fingers, and she arched her back, whimpering. "There's one tattoo that's for really brave people," I whispered, circling her nipple with my finger. Addy whimpered, her hands gripping my sides as her skin raised in a spiderweb pattern over her breast. I gave her tender nipple another pinch, then flooded the pleasure in, replacing the pain, and her fingers dug into me urgently.

Hastily, I undid the button on Addy's jeans, and she helped me push them down her hips, her panties following quickly. I drew a line of stars along her hip, and she squirmed underneath me until a fresh wave of pleasure washed over her, leaving her breathless. I dipped my fingers down lower, and she moaned when I brushed her clit, arching into my hand. She was so wet, I groaned, my dick pulsing. I sent that desire into her instead, watching as she writhed underneath me, eyes half-closed and lips parted in pleasure.

I captured her bottom lip, sucking it into my mouth as my fingers slid inside her. Her pussy clamped around me, slick with her need, and I swallowed her moan, plunging my tongue into her mouth. I slid my fingers in and out, and she rocked against my hand, whimpering desperately. I curled my fingers in, pressing against the sensitive bundle of nerves inside of her. Addy's nails dug into my sides, and she bit my bottom lip, sending a jolt of heat straight to my cock, nearly making me burst. I channelled it into her instead, and she cried out, her pussy clamping down on my fingers as she came apart underneath me, soaking my hand. My fingers continued to stroke as she panted, not letting up until she was good and satiated.

Her hands released their hold on my sides, as she moved to the fly of my jeans, undoing them deftly. I groaned when they slid down my hips, and my dick sprang up, now only trapped by the fabric of my boxers. Addy pulled those down too, and when her hand wrapped around my shaft, I thought I might die. The drug-like quality of her skin seemed to intensify tenfold, and I saw stars as she stroked along my length, moaning low in my throat when she squeezed. I felt her hand drop away, and my hunger for her punched into my chest, but she only dipped her fingers into herself briefly before grasping me once more, her fingers now slick on my shaft. Addy stroked my entire length, sliding her hand up and down, and my arms shook as I tried not to collapse on top of her. Her free hand gripped my tender shoulder, squeezing it tightly before dragging her nails roughly down my chest.

I came apart in her hand with a moan, spilling out in a hot stream across her stomach. Her hand continued to stroke me until I was completely spent. I kissed her again, feeling light-headed and completely at her mercy. Interestingly, I tasted a little tang of guilt on her lips, and I pressed my forehead against hers briefly before shifting off the chair. I grabbed a few wipes from one of the drawers and helped clean off her stomach, giving her a wry smile as she chewed her lip.

"You know, none of us are expecting anything from you," I told her gently as I pulled my pants back on. "We're just happy if you're happy." She was still biting her lip, clearly not believing me. I picked her shirt up off the floor and handed it to her. "Look, none of us were ever going to have a typical relationship," I explained. "Just the fact that you're willing to be here is enough. If you want to do something more with any of us, no one is going to mind. I promise." I smiled. It might feel like one of those lies people told to someone they were afraid of losing, but ours was such an unusual circumstance that it didn't really fall within conventional rules.

I ran my hand down her neck as she processed this, my fingers catching on something rough. The skin on Addy's left shoulder was dimpled, the scars of a burn long healed. I brushed over it gently, and her gaze dropped to the floor. "I saw a house on fire when you went inside my head," I told her quietly, tracing the outline of her scar. "Were you inside when it happened?" She nodded, biting her lip.

"My mother went insane and burned our house down with us inside," Addy told me, her voice barely a whisper. "A neighbour heard me crying and ran inside. He saved me, but he couldn't save my dad." Her eyes lifted to mine, and I could feel the guilt radiating off of her. "I think I drove her crazy with whatever runs in my skin, just like I've done with everyone else I've cared about."

I pressed my hand against her, pulling some of the pain out of her heart. "You didn't mean to hurt anyone. None of it is your fault, you know," I told her softly. "And you won't hurt any of us, I promise." Her face lightened a bit, but her eyes were still a little sad.

"Just so you know, I like... whatever this is," Addy told me, pulling her shirt over her head. I briefly glimpsed my name, just barely visible over her ribs, before her shirt fell to cover it. "You all make me feel... really fucking good." I smiled and kissed her, glad she wasn't overthinking anymore.

"Good. Besides, this is the happiest any of us have been for years. Including Cain, believe it or not." I smirked, making her laugh.

Maybe someday I could sign all our names across her ribs.

Chapter Sixteen

Piper

Time was tricky for me. For most people, it flowed one way, past to present to future. I tended to bounce around a little, my thoughts from the future and my thoughts from the present jumbling up into one big mess, so I had to work very hard to keep things straight. Some days were better than others, and time for the most part would stay still. On those days, I could get out of bed, I could venture outside, and maybe even make some money with the odd fortune or two. On the bad days, though, I had a hard time sorting out what was real and what wasn't, or what was going to be real at some point in the future, but didn't apply to now.

My great-grandmother was a fortune-teller, as were most of the women in my family. It was a common way for them to make money back then, but I didn't know for sure if anyone else had a gift quite like mine. I think mine was broken, a curse more than a gift. See, in my family's culture, only women were born with the gift, not men.

My birth was a mistake from the start. My mother got knocked up by an outsider, someone not from our community. Her mother shunned her for this and kicked her out of the house when she was only seventeen years old. Her grandmother took her in and for a while, everything was okay. But even as a child, there was something not quite right with me, and I would say things and know things that frightened people.

My great-grandmother realized that I had the Sight, and she gave my mother enough money to get us to America, where she thought we'd both be safe. If the rest of the family found out about me, they would have killed us both.

We lived a dirt-poor life together for a long time, but my mother never quite recovered from the pain her family had caused her. I saw her death coming long before it happened, so by the time it came about, I'd already finished grieving for her. I was on my own after that.

I'd travelled for a few years, letting the wind push me through different cities. Sometimes, I'd stumbled into luck, but more often than not, I'd found my way into trouble. My curse only seemed to get worse as I got older, and my mind felt like it was starting to fracture when I stumbled upon Cain. My dreams had brought me to this town, that and a tugging feeling in the centre of my chest, like I was a fish being reeled in. I'd been drinking at a bar one night, and someone caught me trying to lift their wallet. They were kicking the ever-loving shit out of me in the back alley when Cain had appeared out of the darkness, grabbing them off of me and tossing them aside like they weighed nothing. I'd known immediately that Cain was the person I'd come here to find.

Of course, it took two months of me following him around and refusing to leave, for him to finally accept that I was here to stay. For a while after that, my mind stayed whole. It was almost a year later when I began to feel that tug again, but this time I stayed still, and the tug reeled in Austin to us. He just appeared one evening on our doorstep, broken and bloody and unable to speak. I didn't think he'd spoken to another person in a long, long time. Cain warmed up to him faster, because it was clear that he needed us desperately. We worked on teaching him how to be human, which wasn't easy at first. Even now, he understood the basics, but societal constraints were harder for him to grasp. That was why Cain gave him so many rules. For instance, I would often wake up and find Austin in my bed, curled up beside me. I didn't know what had brought him there—if it was loneliness or just the cold—but we had to explain to him that some people didn't like waking up with someone in their beds. I thought, in a lot of ways, I was a poor example for him, so I left it to Wyatt and Cain to explain a lot of those things.

After the tug brought us to Wyatt, I thought that might mean our little group was complete. We were all so fucked up in so many different ways, but lumped together we could almost pass as one functional person. It wasn't exactly perfect, but it was way better than it had been before, at least. Of course, there was one key aspect that was missing from our lives, but for the most part, we each took care of that in our own way.

I knew that Wyatt and Cain would sometimes go out on their own and hook up with girls they'd meet at a club or the bar. In my travels, I'd have the occasional tryst with someone I'd meet on one of my good days. I was not sure what Austin got up to. After he came to live with us, he'd rarely venture outside anymore, likely because of what had happened to drive him here in the first place. Occasionally, if the mood struck us, we'd fool around a bit together, and I thought that was the most companionship he'd had for a long time. There was just one rule: we never brought someone back to the studio. While one of us alone might pass as somewhat normal for at least a couple of hours, we definitely stuck out as a group, so it was best to leave the outsiders, well, outside.

So, when the tug came again, and our little spider found her way to us, it was like seeing the sun after living for years in darkness. It was a wonder any of us could function, even Cain, the most stoic of us all, when Addy was in the room. The moment I kissed her, I felt more clear than I'd ever had before. I was rooted in the present, and all I could see was her face, etched with the same pain as all of ours, made to fit perfectly in the little space left empty in our hearts.

I will admit, having something so tempting living under the same roof was tricky, especially given my problems with time. I'd wake up some mornings and forget she'd already arrived, or quite the opposite, I would forget we'd only spoken once before. My little spider was woven into my mind and tangled in my heart like I'd already known her for years, even though it hadn't happened yet.

It was easy for me to forget that she was still in the present, and this was all still very new and strange for her.

CHAPTER SEVENTEEN

Addison

I went back to my apartment the next day, and the day after that, before I finally just started calling the police department instead and saving myself the trip. I didn't know if there was some kind of conspiracy against me, or if the people working this case were just impressively slow, but it seemed like I would be homeless until at least the end of the week.

Cain, thankfully, had stopped actively trying to force me out of the house and appeared resigned to the fact that I would be here for a while. To make it up to him, I went out and picked up a couple of things to make dinner for everyone that night. I wasn't the world's greatest cook by any means, but I knew my way around a kitchen. Since none of the guys seemed to care about what they put into their mouths, I opted for spaghetti and meatballs, which was a universal crowd-pleaser.

I was still trying to pin down everyone's schedules, which had no discernible pattern as far as I could tell, so I just aimed for dinner to be in the evening, when I assumed at least one of them would be available. I managed to catch Cain and Wyatt and lure them to the table at the same time, and they dug into the food like it was the first time they'd eaten in weeks. Honestly, it might've been judging by the state of their fridge.

"Would Austin like any?" I asked Wyatt between bites. I hadn't seen him this afternoon, and I wasn't sure if he was in the studio or upstairs in his room.

"Austin doesn't really eat much," he replied, shrugging, but I noticed the look he shot Cain, so there must be a little more to that than he was willing to share. There were plenty of leftovers in the fridge anyway, if he did feel like eating later on.

Midway through the meal, Piper breezed in and looked surprised to see us at the table. He looked quite pleased with himself, walking over and snagging a bite off my plate. I smacked him with my fork, pointing to the stove. "There's plenty. Go get your own," I told him. He gave me a cheeky wink and sauntered over to grab a plate. Wyatt was watching him, one eyebrow raised.

"What did you get up to today?" Wyatt asked him, and Cain checked him out as well.

"I went to the bar on campus." Piper smirked, and both guys perked up with noticeable interest.

"And?" Cain prompted, but Piper was clearly enjoying himself and chose to dish up and return to the table before answering.

"And-" Piper stuck a hand in his back pocket and pulled out a large wad of bills, which he dropped on the table with a satisfying thud. If I had to guess, there was at least $600 in his little stack. Wyatt's jaw dropped, and he slapped Piper on the back. Cain reached out and grabbed the bills, counting through them.

"Wow Piper, this must be your best haul yet," Cain mused, looking proud of him. Piper looked pretty proud of himself as well, leaning back in his chair and shooting me a wink. It was almost unnerving when Piper was this coherent. He had a devilish look in his eyes, which were sharper and more clear than I'd ever seen them.

"Sorry, were you bartending?" I asked, and the guys laughed. Well, forgive me for assuming Piper might've had a normal job.

"No one would ever hire Piper to be responsible for booze," Cain told me, smirking at Piper. "No, he's a pool shark. He cons the college kids into pool games, pretending he's drunk. They bet big, and he collects." Oh, well, that does make more sense than him bartending. I imagined that he'd forget he was working pretty quickly and start drinking right from the bottles behind the bar.

"I thought people only bet on that kind of thing in the movies," I mused, grabbing my plate and sticking it in the sink. "Do all of you know how to play?"

Cain and Wyatt both nodded. "Austin is the best at it. Then it goes Cain, Piper when he's sober, me, and Piper when he's drunk." Wyatt laughed, and Piper shook his head indignantly, his mouth full of pasta.

"I'm better than both of you, drunk or sober," he protested. "Austin is the best, but he can't bluff for shit, so he's useless as a pool shark." He sighed like this was a personal tragedy.

"Have you ever played?" Wyatt asked me, clearing his and Cain's plates and sticking them in the sink as well.

I shook my head. "Not really. I might've played once or twice in my life, that's it." I shrugged.

"Let's play a round," Cain suggested, catching all of us off guard. "We've got the table downstairs. And then I can prove to this idiot that I'm better." He smirked at Piper, who stood up and puffed out his chest.

"Challenge accepted," he announced, grabbing his plate and walking downstairs with it. I laughed and followed after him, the other boys at my heels.

Cain and Wyatt pulled the table out from the wall and started setting up, while Piper and I got some drinks from the bar. I'd picked up some plastic cups, so those of us so inclined to civility could drink from something other than the bottle. Piper poured me some rum, taking the bottle for himself with a grin. The other guys stuck with beers, and I watched them argue over breaking and who was on who's team.

"I'll take Addy," Piper announced, and I gave him an incredulous look. "Don't worry, love, I've got this." He smirked, taking a swig from the bottle. He started us off terribly by losing the coin toss, so Cain got to break. I took a sip of my drink, trying to recall every pool scene I'd watched in movies, but most wouldn't help me unless I needed to beat one of them to death with a pool cue.

Cain sunk a couple on the break, and he sunk one more before it was our turn. Piper took it first, sinking three in a row before Wyatt could go. He was feeling very cocky, putting his arm around my waist as he took another drink, watching Wyatt fumble and swear, kicking the wall behind him. *My turn now, I guess.* I grabbed the cue from Piper, trying to mimic their stances and balancing the stick on my knuckles awkwardly.

"Here, love, try angling just a bit this way," Piper murmured in my ear. He was leaning over me, his hip pressing me against the table, moving my hands into a better position. It was such a cliché, I had to bite my cheek to not laugh, but I had to admit, something about Piper's confidence was giving me butterflies. I hit the ball, sending it flying into the one I'd been aiming for, but because of the angle, it bounced right and caught a second one, landing them both in the corner pocket.

"Ha!" I exclaimed, and Wyatt pretended to pout. We were winning now—I *think*—and Cain took a few minutes, considering the table with a scowl. Piper slipped his hand around me again, moving it lower this time to give my ass a rough squeeze. I smacked his chest playfully, but the look in his eyes made my face hot. Hand still gripping my ass, he pulled me against him, just holding me close for a moment before Cain took his turn and it was ours again. I could swear, sometimes Piper looked at me with such a familiar gaze, it was like he'd known me for years.

Piper sank two more, leaving us with only the 8-ball left. I was not in a good position to hit it without knocking at least one other ball into the pocket. I studied the table for a minute before setting myself up in an awkward position, the pool cue forced into my left hand in order to get it at the right angle.

"There's a trick to this one." Piper smiled. He put his hands on my hips and lifted me up so I was sitting on the edge of the pool table. "Now hold it behind your back like this," he instructed, pressing between my legs and wrapping his arms around me, positioning the cue the way he wanted. My face felt hot, and the grin he shot me told me he knew exactly what he was doing. I narrowed my eyes at him, putting my focus on hitting the stupid ball. He was right though, it looked silly, but it did allow me a better angle, and I sunk the 8-ball with a small cry of victory. Wyatt laughed as Cain swore, tossing the pool cue aside.

"I need a smoke," Cain muttered, stalking out of the basement in a huff. Wyatt slapped Piper on the back, shaking his head and still chuckling.

"I'll go see what Austin's up to. Maybe he'd like to put you in your place." He smirked, leaving Piper and me alone. I was still sitting on the lip of the table, and Piper handed me my drink, so I didn't need to move. If anything, his confident swagger was more pronounced now, and he took a hearty swig of rum while I sipped mine, watching the bracelets slide up his wrist as he drank. He stepped close again, moving in between my legs. I shifted, my thighs opening wider to accommodate him. Hunger practically radiated off of him, making the air around us thick and heady. He tipped my chin up and captured my lips, his hands already sliding up my shirt. I felt the charms on his bracelets drift along my back, and he had my bra unhooked before I even realized what he was doing.

"They're going to be back any second," I whispered against his lips. I felt him smile under my lips as his fingers grazed along my breasts, making me shiver as heat rushed to my core. I could feel how hard he was through his jeans, and he rubbed against me, making me groan.

"Would you like that?" he murmured, kissing along my jaw, his fingers teasing my nipples until I arched against him with a whimper. "Maybe I'll just take you right here on this table, and they can gather around and watch." Another shiver of pleasure curled down my spine, and he grabbed my hips, grinding me against him. He kissed me again before I could answer, and his hands slipped back up my shirt.

I heard footsteps on the stairs, and someone cleared their throat as they walked in. Piper pulled away from me abruptly, and I moved to adjust my shirt—he'd somehow re-hooked my bra while we'd been making out.

"Alright Piper, that's enough of that. It's time for a re-match," Cain announced. Piper lifted me off the table, giving me one last kiss, a cocky grin on his face. I moved over to lean against one of the chairs, letting the guys play this round. My heart was pounding in my chest. Would he have actually fucked me on that table if I had said yes? He met my eyes from across the table as the others argued about who would break.

Something in his eyes made me wonder how he knew that the next time he offered, I would say yes.

Chapter Eighteen

Addison

It had been nearly three weeks since I'd sort of accidentally moved in with the guys. Every day I spent close to an hour on the phone with an assortment of unhelpful people, asking why my apartment was still a goddamn crime scene, and it seemed like no one had any actual answers for me. Finally, I talked someone into at least letting me inside to get more of my things, and another officer escorted me in and watched me shove a bunch of my clothes and my few remaining un-destroyed personal items in a bag to take back to the building. Wyatt came with me again, and at his suggestion, I grabbed a few of the remaining kitchen supplies to bolster the sad little collection they had in their own bare cupboards.

Cain still seemed annoyed by my presence in general, but I'd like to think he was beginning to come around. One day, I returned from the lab to find that they had rearranged the basement. Someone had stapled sheets to the ceiling in one corner, and inside I found a mattress, ironically bare, and a worn-looking dresser for my clothes. Someone else, I suspected Austin, had strung faerie lights along the perimeter of the wall of sheets, adding a soft glow to my little cave.

I went out that evening and got a couple sets of sheets and some new pillows, and moved my bags of stuff out of Cain's room. I tried to thank him, but he just grunted and slammed the door in my face, which I took as an acknowledgement. My little room was a lot less impressive than my old room in my apartment, but it was cozy, and private, and didn't have the stench of death in it.

I fell into an easy routine with the guys, finding my own space within the rhythm of the house. I woke up at 7 a.m. most days, so I could get dressed and ready for work in the basement before heading up to the kitchen. Wyatt was normally up late working, and he'd sleep until at least 8 a.m., or later in the morning. Coffee was first on his agenda, which he now would drink in the kitchen with me instead of out on the fire escape.

I took over grocery shopping from Piper permanently, because I was worried I might get a vitamin deficiency with the sheer lack of produce in the house. Now, we had bread and fruit for breakfast, plus supplies for proper dinners. Austin, whose sleep seemed to vary depending on the weather and his work schedule, would always scramble downstairs to say goodbye before I left for the day. Most days, he would just scoop me up in a hug, but occasionally he would decide to kiss me until I was breathless. I still hadn't figured out what guided his decision day to day. At first, I'd been a little embarrassed when he'd done that in front of Wyatt, but Wyatt just laughed, so I stopped worrying about it.

PDA in general didn't seem to affect anyone in the house, except maybe Cain, but he just scowled at everything, anyway. Cain would normally wander out just as I was leaving the house, always under the guise of locking the door behind me, since I didn't have my own key yet. Every day, he seemed to find some reason to touch me, just a bit. Maybe it was helping me with my coat, passing me my purse, or even brushing an invisible speck of dust off my cheek. That was his version of PDA, or maybe he just needed one last fix of the spell my skin wove before I left for the day.

After work, I'd either head to the market nearby or go straight home to the studio. Unless he was with a client, Austin always greeted me at the door when I arrived, giving me a big hug and helping me carry in the groceries, if there were any. Some days Piper met me at the door, and he always looked a little confused at first until he touched my cheek. Then his eyes would clear up, and he'd kiss me with a fervour that made my knees weak before escorting me inside.

Sometimes I would cook dinner, because I personally liked to eat, and I would make enough for anyone who wandered in. Other times Cain would already be busy by the stove, and I would let him do his thing. Maybe it was the consistent groceries, or maybe he also realized that I at least needed regular meals, but he took great care in the dinners he prepared, and it seemed like he did know how to cook pretty well.

Cain and I would sit in silence and eat most nights, maybe exchanging a word or two, but it was mostly me driving any sort of conversation. I think he would make a good monk, since he could probably sit for years in silent contemplation. Wyatt would wander in if he had finished work or was taking a break, and he would grab a couple of bites and give me a quick kiss before disappearing downstairs. Austin rarely joined us for meals, and I didn't think I'd seen him eat more than once or twice since I'd arrived. I wasn't sure if he even needed to eat, or if he just ate things that weren't... found in our fridge. I preferred not to think about it. Sometimes Piper would find us in the kitchen, and he'd always be pleasantly surprised with the food. I figured out pretty quickly that he wouldn't know right away which meal we were even eating.

Evening activities varied from day to day, but since I now lived in their common living room space, I often participated in whatever they got into. Most nights, at least one or two of them would come down and have a beer, talking shit or describing their work for the day. I'd join in, and Wyatt in particular seemed fascinated with my work with the spiders in the lab. He'd ask me a lot of questions about my paper, which made me happy. Some nights, if there were at least three of us, we'd play cards or, sometimes, pool. Piper, depending on the day, was either amazing at cards or absolutely terrible. Any games of chance were his strong suit, but if he was having an off day, his mind would wander, and he'd start reading things in our cards instead of playing the game.

I couldn't be sure, but there might've been some kind of challenge going on that I wasn't aware of. It felt like most nights, there was a race to be the one to sit with me on the couch. Austin was normally the winner because, sometimes, he'd camp out on the couch while we ate dinner, waiting for us to come downstairs. He would pull me into his lap and tickle my neck as we had our drinks, his hands drifting across my body as we talked. Occasionally Wyatt would beat him there, and he was much more subtle about it. Normally just an arm over my shoulder, or tracing little patterns along my thigh.

Piper might've also been in on the game, but if he won, I had to be careful. He would either forget or just not care that the other guys were around. His hands would sneak under my shirt, or roam over my lap as if they had minds of their own. Nobody ever said anything, though. In fact, nobody seemed to care. Occasionally, I would look over and catch them watching with hungry eyes, but they all seemed to have agreed that jealousy was off the table, and that was nice. I liked all my guys, even Cain, and I didn't want them acting like cavemen over this.

My space seemed to be the off-limits zone for the most part, and no one went inside except me. I thought Austin might try one of his late-night visits again once I moved downstairs, but I guess Cain had scared him off of that. I was grateful because I needed the sleep and the time to myself. Sometimes, we'd stay up too late goofing around, and I was left with only a few hours before I had to get up for work.

I was happy in this new rhythm, and I'd never realized just how lonely I'd been before I met them.

Inevitably, because I had been staying there so long, my hormones caught up with me. One morning, I woke up irritable and snippy, ready to fight with anyone who crossed my path. Poor Wyatt was shocked when I snapped at him for not making enough coffee and didn't understand why I didn't want to cuddle with him at the breakfast table. Realizing what was coming, I stayed home from work, hiding in my little makeshift space and snarling when my laptop refused to work fast enough. I needed a hot water bottle, an Advil, and some goddamn chocolate, none of which were available in this godforsaken man-cave of a house.

Stalking upstairs into the kitchen, I groaned as pain began to ripple across my abdomen, causing me to double over at the kitchen counter while I waited for the water to boil in the kettle. Cain was the one who found me there. He seemed to have a sixth sense for when I was vulnerable, or just not in the fucking mood and liked to appear, looking annoyed, ready to push my temper to its limits.

"What's wrong with you?" he demanded, stomping toward me. I looked up from my bent-over position and glowered at him.

"I'm fucking dying, just leave me alone, alright?" I growled, shutting my eyes as the pain seemed to amplify, travelling down my thighs.

"Are you okay?" he asked, stepping closer, his hands running over my back.

"I'm fine!" I hissed. "Have none of you been around a woman for longer than a month before?" I tried to straighten up but failed, and gave up on my hopes for tea, turning off the burner and shuffling back toward the stairs.

"Hold on," Cain snapped, grabbing my shoulder and spinning me around. "Are you - is this..." He frowned, making a gesture that only mimes could interpret.

"I'm on my goddamn period, okay?" I shouted at him, wincing and dropping down to the floor, the cramps becoming unbearable. God forbid I could get through this pain without suffering from the embarrassment of having to announce it to the entire household.

"Well, Jesus Christ, just spit it out next time," he snapped and scooped me up into his arms. Instead of walking to my intended destination of the basement, he took me back to his room, and I groaned and rolled onto my stomach as soon as he set me down on the bed, wishing I could just pass out already.

"Let me help," he ordered, slipping his hand underneath me until it was pressing against my lower abdomen. A blissful pulse of heat radiated out of his hand, soaking into my tender abdomen and relaxing the muscles that were currently screaming in agony. I actually moaned out loud, relaxing into his hand, and the rest of my body gave out, surrendering to the warmth of his fingers.

"Oh my god, thank you," I whimpered, feeling him lay down on the bed next to me. Carefully, he pulled me over toward him, turning me until I was on my side, pressed against him with his hand on my stomach.

"You have scared every person in this house today," he told me bluntly, and I sighed, too sore to care about that right now.

"I'll apologize tomorrow," I murmured.

"You know, there are other things that can help with cramps," Cain told me gently. "And there are several people in this house who would be more than willing to help you. You just have to ask nicely." I grumbled, and he chuckled in my ear. He was being so... weirdly kind to me today. I wasn't used to sensitive Cain.

"Help how exactly?" I asked, my eyes closing as I relaxed under the heat of his hand.

"I've read that orgasms help with cramps," he told me softly, and I sputtered out a laugh.

"No one is going to sleep with me right now," I replied tiredly. "It'd be like fucking a badger."

"You're all bark, you're too tired to bite." Cain smirked, and his free hand slipped under the waistband of my pyjama bottoms and inside my panties.

I tensed, but at the first brush of his fingers against my sensitive clit, I practically melted into his arms. "Oh god," I whimpered, and he took that as encouragement, circling and teasing the tender bundle of nerves with a slow, almost torturous precision. It felt so good, the pleasure distracting me from the pain as my pussy thrummed with need, spasming as small sparks of heat pulsed through it. "Fuck Cain, oh my god!" I whimpered, writhing in his arms as my orgasm ripped through me, taking my breath away.

"Well, it sure took the fight out of you at least," Cain teased, but I was too worn out to care. I let Cain be my human heating pad as I drifted off to sleep in his arms, my cramps already a distant memory.

Chapter Nineteen

Piper

The moon needed to stop moving before I fell off the Earth. I was on my bed, I think. But I could see the moon through the ceiling, or maybe it was the window. Was that the moon even? It felt hot against my eyes. Maybe it was daytime already. What time was it?

I rolled, trying to orient myself, and the world threw me in the air, hard enough for me to land on the ceiling. I sat up, or down? And maybe it was the floor. My stomach hurt. I wasn't sure if it was hunger or death clawing at my insides. I couldn't even remember the last time I'd eaten. It depended on what day it was today.

I crawled until I reached the door and pulled myself up, trying to find the doorknob. I couldn't remember going to bed, or when I'd put on this shirt. It was red. Was red Wednesday, or Monday? *Shit.* The doorknob reformed itself in my hand, and I stumbled outside, the moon—or the sun—still shifting the Earth too much for comfort.

I followed the sounds of voices down the hall and climbed up the stairs. Or, down the stairs, it was down from here, I think. One of the stairs jumped free, and I floated away before the house slammed into my back. "Jesus Christ Piper, not again!" I heard a voice call me. Was that Cain? I looked over at his face as it shifted from old to young to ageless, his eyes smoking as they fell out of his head. Arms hooked under my shoulders, pulling me out of the water. How long had I been under? My lungs burned with the need for air.

"He must be high again," someone told me or Cain, and my chest heaved, and an ocean's worth of water came pouring out of my mouth. I heaved again, and more water came. It wasn't ocean water though, it was from the bathtub he'd tried to drown me in. Was that me? I couldn't remember. Someone had drowned, or had tried to drown, or would be drowned.

"What is that?! Is he dying?" My little spider, her voice was like a song in a rainstorm. Was she still here? She hadn't left yet. That was good. She couldn't leave. We had to save her. I heaved a third time, and this time a small spider came out along with the bath water. Poor thing, he'd drowned her, too. Maybe the Pain-Eater could help... but he only ate pain, not death. Was he dead, too? He had tried to die before. Or had that happened yet? What day was it again?

My little spider—the live one, not the dead one, *yet?* —she was reaching for me. Her hand touched my face, and the whole world flipped upside down, or no, right side up. The kitchen was back in focus, although it was a lot more wet than it normally was. My head hurt. Had I hit it on something? Cain knelt down beside me, and oh boy, he looked mad.

"What did you take this time, Piper?" He burned my eyes when I looked at him, so I looked at my little spider instead.

She was soft and gentle. I gripped her hand tightly to stay on the ground.

"I didn't take anything, I don't think..." I frowned, my mind floating in broken-up pieces in my skull.

"You just fell down the stairs and threw up about a gallon of something all over the kitchen!" Cain snapped. "Not to mention, you've been muttering about drowning and dead spiders. You're telling me you did that sober?"

"I remember... I remember going to sleep," I muttered, rubbing my eyes. "But something bad tugged at me and pulled me out. Something bad is going to happen... or did happen? Maybe both, I think." I sighed.

"Well, you fell down the fucking stairs. Was that the bad thing?" Wyatt asked, sopping up the mess on the floor with a towel. "Man, what the fuck is this? Is this water?"

"It looked like you had nearly drowned," Addy told me, her voice pulling me back just as I'd started to fall away again. I hooked my arms around her and pulled her down into my lap. She'd keep me from falling.

"I did. He was drowning me in the tub. I couldn't breathe, and no one came to save me. Then he just stopped," I murmured. "I woke up on the floor. I coughed up so much water, I thought it would never stop coming out."

"What the fuck did you just say?" Cain asked in a low voice. It wasn't me who drowned, *that's right*. It was a little boy, a small child named Cain. They should've named him Abel. His brother was the killer, not him.

"It was you," I whispered. "He's coming back, Cain, and he wants to drown us. He's going to take our little spider and hold her under until she stops kicking, just like you." I gripped Addy until my knuckles turned white. He couldn't take her.

I'd fall away again, and then I'd never be able to get back to Earth. The tethers were getting so weak now, I wouldn't hold on much longer on my own.

"Piper, you're hurting her," Wyatt warned, grabbing my arm. I loosened my grip just a bit and felt my little spider gasp in a breath. She wasn't drowning yet, not yet. I stroked her hair, humming a tune she sang to me... or not her, someone else? Who sang that song? Had I met them yet?

"How do you know he's coming?" Cain demanded, drawing me back to the kitchen. It was so damp here. Why was the floor wet?

"I don't know who, or why, or when. I just know what will happen, and that it can't happen. He wants your toys, Cain. You know he doesn't like it when you have toys. He's going to play with them and break them, and we won't get the pieces back together this time." I groaned, my stomach clenching and my head pounding. I felt my little spider rubbing my face, whispering to me.

"Cain, do you know what the fuck he's going on about?" Wyatt asked, kicking the towel by his foot in frustration. "This feels like one of those things we shouldn't ignore."

"I think... I think he's saying that my brother has found me," Cain growled.

CHAPTER TWENTY

Addison

As Friday nights went, ours ended up being pretty wild. It had started out normal enough. I'd stopped at the market on the way home from the lab and picked up some steaks at Cain's request. After I'd handed them off, I stole away to shower and change into more comfortable clothes. I still used Cain's shower in his on-suite, and he didn't seem to mind. It had the best water pressure in the house, and it was less likely that one of the guys would come in and surprise me there. Feeling much more relaxed in my sweats and an old tee shirt, I returned to the kitchen and found Wyatt already sitting at the table, two beers in his hand. He handed one to me with a smile, and we both sat and watched as Cain busied himself around the kitchen.

I would have offered to help, but I knew better than to disrupt him while he worked. He was a solo cook, and he'd get pretty nasty if he had to dodge around anyone while he worked. He seemed to instinctively know how to cook things to the perfect temperature. I never saw him use a thermometer or set a timer. I bet he would make a talented chef.

He even enjoyed cursing out other people in the kitchen. Unfortunately, he'd probably end up stabbing someone if he was working with knives all the time, so maybe cooking was best left as a hobby. Once he'd declared the steaks done, we'd all grabbed a plate and were having a perfectly lovely dinner when Piper had suddenly thrown himself down the stairs.

He landed in a heap at the bottom, and his eyes were so glassy and pupils so dilated I'd thought for a moment that he was dead. Cain sprang out of his chair and ran over to him, swearing and demanding to know what he'd taken. I wondered if, maybe, he'd O.D.'d before. I knew he wasn't exactly careful with his recreational substances. Though, I guess, it would be hard to be if you constantly forgot you'd taken something and took more.

Piper was trying to tell us something, but none of it made any sense. It was just a jumble of random words strung together. Then his lips turned a terrifying shade of blue, and he started gasping like he couldn't breathe. Cain hauled him up by his armpits, trying to sit him up, and then he just began heaving. It was like we'd just fished him out of the lake. Buckets of water poured out of his mouth as he emptied his lungs and his stomach, gasping for air. Wyatt swore and jumped up, running to grab some towels for the mess, while I just stared in horror. After another heave of water, I saw a little spider, legs curled up and on its back, floating in the puddle he'd created in the middle of the kitchen. Had he eaten a spider? My skin prickled as I watched the little body drift across the floor.

Gingerly, I stepped across the spreading puddle, moving to Piper's side as Cain slammed his back, trying to dislodge the last of the water. I touched Piper's cheek gently, and I watched as the clouds over his eyes faded, and he seemed to actually see me in front of him for the first time. His pupils were still huge and looked so horribly frightened. He grabbed my hand and pinned it against his face like it was the only thing holding him together. Cain was still trying to get some answers, asking him what happened, still convinced he was high on something. But his eyes were clear now, and I'd never seen someone look so terrified.

"I remember... I remember going to sleep," he muttered, rubbing his eyes. "But something bad tugged at me and pulled me out. Something bad is going to happen... or did happen? Maybe both, I think." Piper looked so tired. I didn't remember seeing him yesterday at all. How long had he been out of it? Suffering in this weird dream state by himself?

"Well, you fell down the fucking stairs, was that the bad thing? Man, what the fuck is this? Is this water?" Wyatt was trying in vain to sop up the mess, which was spreading toward the cabinets. I could still see the spider floating away, and the image gave me a chill.

"It looked like you nearly drowned," I whispered, trying to figure out how that would be possible. Unless he'd shoved his head in a bucket, or the sink maybe, there were no bathtubs that he could have slipped into or fallen asleep in. I yelped in surprise when he grabbed me, pulling me down onto his lap like I was a lifejacket and he was alone in the ocean.

His arms were shaking as they wrapped around me. "I did. He was drowning me in the tub. I couldn't breathe, and no one came to save me. Then he just stopped," he murmured. "I woke up on the floor. I coughed up so much water I thought it would never stop coming out." My heart ached as I stroked his cheek, trying to soothe him as best I could. He wasn't making sense anymore, and I tried to pull him back to Earth. I saw Austin's head poke out, drawn downstairs by the noise. He looked like we had woken him up, his face a mask of concern.

"What the fuck did you just say?" Cain was snarling behind me, and I shot him a glare. Now was not the time to be yelling at Piper.

"It was you," Piper whispered, and his eyes widened into saucers. "He's coming back, Cain, and he wants to drown us. He's going to take our little spider and hold her under until she stops kicking, just like you." My lungs gave a little squeak as Piper's arms tightened around my chest, squeezing the air out of me. I squirmed, but he was holding on so tight I couldn't break free of his hold.

Wyatt was down beside him quickly, tugging on his arms. "Piper, you're hurting her," he snapped, and Piper finally released his death grip so I could gasp air back into my lungs. He stroked my hair gently, humming a song I didn't recognize, his eyes unfocused and cloudy. Cain was still trying to interrogate him about this mysterious person he thought was going to kill me, and Wyatt stayed close by, ready to pull me away if Piper decided to crush me again.

"I don't know who, or why, or when. I just know what will happen, and that it can't happen. He wants your toys, Cain. You know he doesn't like it when you have toys. He's going to play with them and break them, and we won't get the pieces back together this time." Piper shook, and I petted his hair gently, trying to get him to calm down.

I stroked his cheek, feeling his tears dampen my hand. "It's okay," I murmured. "It's going to be okay." He closed his eyes and curled up against me, his face twisted in pain.

"Cain, do you know what the fuck he's going on about?" Wyatt asked. He'd stood back up to deal with the mess on the floor, kicking at the towel. "This feels like one of those things we shouldn't ignore." I nodded along with him. This didn't feel like Piper's normal ramblings to me either, and my veins filled with an icy dread.

"I think... I think he's saying that my brother has found me," Cain growled. I stared at him, wide-eyed and confused. He had a brother? He'd never mentioned anything about his family, but no one here really had. I had a feeling none of us had any good things to say about family. Wyatt seemed to know what he was talking about, though, and his lips pressed into a thin line.

"I thought you said that was impossible," he replied quietly, and they shared a quick, wordless exchange. I had a feeling that whatever this was, it wasn't for everyone's ears, at least not right now.

"Austin, can you help me take Piper back upstairs?" I asked, and he bounded over quickly. We'd leave Cain and Wyatt to discuss whatever secrets were threatening us, and I'd press Wyatt for information later on. With Austin's help, I got untangled from Piper's arms, and we got him to his feet, but he was swaying dangerously, like he couldn't find his balance. Austin propped him up on his shoulder for support, and I helped to guide him back upstairs.

Piper's door had been left open, and his room looked like someone had ransacked it. Austin didn't react to the mess, though, so I guess this was just how Piper lived. I pulled his comforter down and helped Austin set Piper on the bed. As soon as he was lying down, Piper started to shake, like he was freezing to death, and it made my heart ache. I crawled over to him and curled up at his side, stroking his arm to try to calm him down. He turned into me and wrapped me in his arms, holding on for dear life. Austin turned off the light, and I expected that he would leave, but instead, he just closed the door and crawled in beside us, tucking himself against my back and pulling the comforter over the three of us.

"I'll stay, just in case," Austin whispered in my ear. Probably for the best, I wouldn't know what I'd do if Piper coughed up any more water or tried to squeeze me to death again. Gradually, his shakes began to slow, and Piper grew quiet as he drifted off to sleep. I heard Austin's breath slow as he too fell asleep behind me, and I tried to settle my own mind so I could get some sleep as well.

I had a fairly restless night, sandwiched between the two guys. I wasn't used to the restricted space they provided, and I found it tricky to get into a comfortable position with the tangle of heavy limbs around me. At some point early in the morning, Piper began mumbling in his sleep, his breath tickling across my face. I couldn't understand what he was saying, but he didn't seem in much distress at least, so I rolled over and tried to fall back to sleep. Piper's arms tightened around me and pulled me flush against him, continuing his nonsensical sleep ramblings into my hair. Eventually, his mumbling trailed off, and I managed to slip into a light doze.

It was late morning when I became aware of a slight movement along my abdomen, Piper's fingers tickling up under my shirt. I ignored him. He moved a lot in his sleep, so this wasn't particularly new. His fingers seemed to always be exploring some part of me, even when he was deep asleep. He brushed along the underside of my breast, and I felt his hard length pressing against my hip. I was still tired from the lack of sleep last night, so I kept my eyes shut, and he seemed content to just touch my skin. I must've started to doze off again when I felt a tugging, and my shirt was being pulled up over my head. Shivering at the rush of cold air against my chest, I sighed when Piper's hands returned to my sides, warming me up.

I gasped when I felt lips graze along my breast, a tongue swirling over my nipple. It couldn't be Piper, who was still pressed firmly up along my back, hands now roving down along my hips. I opened my eyes and could just make out the top of Austin's head poking out from over the covers before it ducked back under, capturing my other breast in his mouth.

"You- you seem to be feeling better this morning," I told Piper, my breath hitching as Austin teased my nipple until it grew hard under his tongue. I felt Piper's breath against my ear as he laughed, his hand slipping deftly under my panties to graze against my sex. Warmth surged to meet his fingers, spurred on by Austin's mouth.

"I was telling Austin how good you tasted," he murmured, his fingers running down along my slit. "I told him he had to try you for himself." Austin looked up at the sound of his name, smiling at me, his eyes hungry as his pupils dilated. Piper pulled his fingers out of my sweats and held them out to Austin, who licked them off like it was a completely ordinary thing for them to do. The look he gave me was purely predatory, and I shivered as Piper reached down to tug my sweats and panties down my thighs. He pulled my shoulder toward him until I was on my back on the bed.

Austin settled between my legs with a grin, and I moaned when his mouth descended on my pussy, his tongue swirling around my clit. Piper kissed me just as enthusiastically, his tongue parting my lips and entering me just as Austin did the same. One of my hands tangled in Austin's hair, my hips bucking as he fucked me with his tongue. My other hand wrapped around Piper, who finished ravishing my mouth and moved to my breasts, teasing and sucking as Austin did the same to my clit. Pressure was building in my core, and I clenched my thighs, trapping Austin between them. This just spurred him on, and his tongue dipped into me again, drawing out a whimper from my throat. I cried out as I came, and still they didn't let up. Austin was sucking my swollen clit mercilessly as I came again not minutes later, soaking the bed with my arousal.

Piper reached for something beside his bed and tossed it to Austin. I watched as he slipped off his pants, exposing his hard cock, which also was pierced, just like the rest of him. He slipped the condom on and climbed back between my legs before hesitating and shooting me a quick look. "Yes," I told him immediately, and he pounced, closing the space between us in a heartbeat. I felt him tease my entrance for only a moment before he sank into me, and I arched, my pussy clamping around him. Austin started to thrust, his cock slick with my desire, and I whimpered as he slammed against my G-spot, sending sparks of pleasure down my spine. Piper was still crouched by my side, enjoying the show. He'd stripped off his pants at some point, and his cock was leaking pre-cum. He was stroking himself, eyes hungry as he watched Austin thrust into me. It was hot to think that he could get off just by watching us, but I had an even better idea.

I caught his eye and beckoned him over. He moved toward me, shifting on the bed until he was close to my face. I opened my mouth invitingly, and he gave me a wicked grin as he slid his cock over my tongue, my hand wrapping around his shaft as my tongue swirled around the tip. He let out a groan and pulled out slowly before plunging back in at the same time as Austin. I tipped back my head and let him fuck my mouth while Austin picked up his pace. They worked in tandem, hands moving along my breasts and teasing my clit until I thought I might burst with pleasure.

I moaned around Piper's cock when I came, my pussy clenching around Austin, and he followed a moment later with a moan of his own. Piper grunted, and I felt him coat the back of my throat. Once spent, Piper fell back down beside me, panting, and Austin crawled up along my other side, resting his head next to mine. His eyes were half closed, and he tucked my hair behind my ear before nuzzling against my neck. Piper kissed my forehead and curled up beside me, pulling the blankets up to cover us.

"Little spider," he murmured, his nickname for me making me smile. He felt clearer now, like the time he'd spent next to me had helped bring him back from wherever his mind drifted during his episodes. We dozed off in our pile of tangled limbs, warm and satiated and safe together.

Chapter Twenty-One

Cain

I needed this to be another one of Piper's damn benders. He just... couldn't be right about this. Wyatt helped clean up the kitchen after Addy and the boys left, and as far as we could tell, it was just water covering our floor. That really didn't make any sense, because we didn't have a fucking bathtub that Piper could've half-drowned himself in. I didn't even think we had a bucket in this place big enough for someone to stick their head inside. I'd seen this sort of thing happen to him before, a couple of times in the past. We'd found snakes in the house every day for a week before Austin had shown up on our doorstep. I remembered staying up all night and watching in horror as a snake slithered out of Piper's mouth while he was lying semi-conscious in bed, his eyes glazed over. Years later, I'd found him in a similar position on the kitchen floor, covered in blood. There was a puddle of it underneath him, but try as I might, I couldn't find a single wound on his body. I took him to the ER that night, and while they pumped him full of fluids, I'd stumbled upon Wyatt in the next bed over, half dead, with bandages covering his arms.

He's going to take our little spider and hold her under until she stops kicking, just like you.

Wyatt was right. I couldn't ignore this one. He knew about my brother Jake, but not by choice. I'd been having one of my… whatever the fuck they were—he called them episodes, but I thought they were migraines—and he'd done his twisted little move with his eyes and taken me away from my body before I could burn the house down. He got pummelled by my memories. I had already been so mad and in so much pain they just exploded, sucking him into the worst parts of my childhood. Wyatt had taken enough of the pain into himself so I could finally calm down, but when he'd set me back in my body, I could see on his face the toll it took on him. We'd both slept for a couple of days after that incident and, while Wyatt had never asked me about what he'd seen, he knew enough to understand that my brother could never discover us here.

Wyatt had gone to bed, sometime early in the morning, but I stayed rooted at the table, unable to close my eyes. I heard some interesting sounds float down from Piper's room, so it appeared that he was feeling somewhat better, at least. Wyatt wandered down, looking exhausted, and started fucking with the coffeemaker as Addy made a sound that had both of us tensing. Wyatt recovered first, grabbing a mug and setting it down on the counter before coming to join me at the table. He gave me a knowing smirk, and I just rolled my eyes. Austin and Piper had really just accepted our new situation with Addy, like it was a normal occurrence. Neither of them seemed to worry at all that this could just be a fleeting moment that would hurt them more after it was over. They lived for the present, while the rest of us were stuck brooding in the past.

He wants your toys, Cain. You know he doesn't like it when you have toys.

I clenched my fists, and Wyatt handed me a cup of coffee when the machine dinged. We sat in silence for a while, true silence since it seemed like the merry trio had finished up for now.

"Could he really have found you?" Wyatt finally asked, looking over at me. I grimaced, staring down into my cup like it would hold the answers for me. I'd been more than careful. Moving across the country, I'd opened a new bank account and stayed off the internet. Our business didn't feature my name anywhere, except the building and the license, which wasn't easy information to access. But he had his ways. I knew that. I had just thought, or really I'd hoped...

"I thought he might be dead," I told Wyatt, grimacing. "It's been over a decade and nothing. So I thought maybe..." I sighed, watching the steam from my coffee shift under my breath. "If he's found me, I need to leave." Wyatt's face was grim, and I pulled out a cigarette, preferring the smoke to the caffeine for the moment. I'd really hoped he was dead...

I should've been more prepared for this, but I'd grown soft and complacent. Happy? Not quite, but close. Close enough that it would hurt more to uproot and leave this time. And now I had additional worries, like what would they do without me?

Wyatt might be okay for a while, but what if he got into one of his dark moods again? Sometimes the pain and the sadness overwhelmed him, and there wasn't anyone to take his pain away like he did with us.

Who would make sure Austin went outside and kept talking to people? He'd slip back into the near-feral state he'd been in when he found us, eating mice and sleeping huddled in a ball under the bed. He would hardly talk when he'd first arrived, just hiss. I got him to talk again, and we'd found him a job he could do to make money for himself, to be human.

Piper needed someone to watch out for him. It was why he'd found me in the first place. He forgot to eat, to breathe, and sometimes whatever he saw in his head was too fucked up, and he'd take too much of something to try to drown it out. Who would watch for that?

Addy could help. She seemed to bring everyone down to earth with her witchy ways. But who would care for her while she cared for everyone else? I made sure she ate, and that she got time to be herself, time alone. If I was gone, would she stop leaving the house too, worrying about the others too much to worry about her own needs?

I couldn't leave them, but I couldn't stay, because I was putting them in more danger if I stayed. *Fuck!* My coffee hissed as it began to boil in my hand, threatening to bubble over just like my rage. The buzzing in my temples jumped an octave, vibrating my teeth and making my eyes sting. Sometimes it got so bad, I thought my skull might just burst, splattering the house with brains and the bees that must be trapped inside.

The buzzing abruptly dissipated, and I heard footsteps on the stairs. Addy appeared on the landing, dressed in one of Piper's tee-shirts, her hair mussed and feet bare. "Good morning." She smiled. "I smelled coffee. Is there any left?"

Wyatt jumped up and grabbed another mug for her, and she came around to sit beside me at the table. He handed her the coffee and stole a quick kiss, grinning as he sat back down. I didn't understand how Addy worked. She said it was her skin that made people crazy, but it felt more like she was sunshine bottled in human form. Somehow, just by her coming into the room, Wyatt seemed happier and the buzzing in my temples was nothing more than a quiet hum. Even the weight in my chest seemed to have lifted. I didn't even think she was aware of what she did. Maybe she had really wanted some coffee, but somehow she'd picked the moment she most needed to arrive, and then she'd sat beside me. She rarely did that, not when Wyatt was around, who was much more friendly.

Her bare legs were nearly touching mine under the table, painfully close. I tried to give Addy her space, as best I could. Everyone else in this damn house grabbed at her and felt her up any chance they could get. Addy didn't seem to mind at all. In fact, she seemed to glow whenever someone touched her, but I figured she might like the space once in a while, so I didn't bother her as the others did. Someone always had to be the responsible adult in this house, and it always ended up being me.

"Should we be worried?" Addy asked me, her fingers wrapped around the mug like she was cold. I shifted over, just a little, and threw off a bit more heat. Maybe she just wanted to sit near me because I was so warm. Sometimes Austin did that, especially in the winter. That seemed to do the trick, her body relaxing a little more beside me.

"About Piper?" Wyatt asked her, shooting me a look. He wouldn't go and talk about my business. I knew that telling her was up to me to handle.

"Yeah, it felt pretty real, the warning, I mean. Should we do something about it?" Addy nodded, looking between Wyatt and me.

"Just don't do anything stupid for the next little while," I said, and she gave me a dirty look. I glared back at her, needing her to take this seriously. "I mean it, don't be running around and hanging out with strangers by yourself." She rolled her eyes.

"I don't do much of that as it is," she replied cooly, sitting up straight. See, why did she have to take everything I said and put an annoying spin on it? No wonder we were always snapping at each other. She had her nose out of joint every time I opened my mouth.

"Maybe one of us can go with you for groceries for a while, so nobody is out by themselves," Wyatt suggested, and Addy seemed to soften a bit.

"Okay, I guess so. But I'm still going to the lab," Addy replied. "I normally just walk there and back when the weather's nice." Fuck, of course, she had work.

"I'll drive you," I offered, regretting the offer as soon as the words left my mouth. She looked at me like I'd proposed marriage or something as ridiculous.

"You want to drive me to work and pick me up every day?" Addy asked incredulously, shifting in her seat. Clearly, she also wasn't looking forward to spending more one-on-one time with me.

"For a while." I shrugged. "Then we can pick up groceries too, if we have to." I took a sip of my coffee as she digested this, chewing on her lip.

"Sure, that would be fine then, if you're okay with it," she replied carefully. I just shrugged and grunted at her, scowling when Wyatt smirked into his mug.

This was going to be a nightmare. If Piper had gotten us worried for nothing, I would shave that fortune-telling twerp's head in his sleep.

Chapter Twenty-Two

Addison

The rest of the weekend brought no more ominous outbursts from Piper, which everyone was thankful for. At Cain's request, we all stayed pretty close to home or, if we had to go out, we went in pairs. Wyatt seemed to have an inkling of who or what Cain was so worried about, but neither of them deigned to share any details with the rest of us, at the moment. Cain never mentioned driving me after the first time on Saturday morning, so when Monday morning came around, I wasn't sure exactly what I was supposed to do.

I got dressed and ready for work like I normally did, but I didn't see Cain when I went up to the kitchen for my coffee. His bedroom door was still shut, and I didn't want to just barge in there and wake him up. I felt like normal Cain was crabby enough. No need to poke the bear first thing in the morning. I waited until it was close to the time I'd be heading out the door to walk and got my jacket and my bag ready, figuring I'd just hoof it, like I usually did.

Just as I was heading out the front door, Cain seemed to appear from out of nowhere and gave me a look that suggested I was insane for not waiting for him. I huffed and adjusted my bag over my shoulder, following my surly driver out to the car. I'd seen it before, parked in the same spot outside the studio, but I'd never ridden in it until today. It was an older black car, some model I didn't recognize, but it looked well-maintained for its age. I hopped in the passenger seat, setting my bag on my lap, and he got in silently beside me, slamming his door shut.

"Do you need directions?" I asked him after he pulled out and turned onto the road. He gave me a sidelong glance and grabbed my bag out of my lap, stowing it in the back seat without asking. I cocked an eyebrow at him but said nothing of the weirdly mom-like behaviour I'd just witnessed.

"Campus is at the end of the road. Science buildings are on the left," he told me, and I stared at him while he just looked at me impatiently.

"I'm not stupid. I looked it up before we left," he told me, and I was so surprised, I laughed. He just rolled his eyes and turned back to the road, content with silence, I guess. But fuck him. I didn't feel like silence. Most of my days were filled with silence until I got back home. I'd like some conversation before I entered my lonely workspace.

"So, you know what building my lab is in?" I asked, seeing just how much research he'd done on my job.

Cain sighed heavily. "Your lab is in the Fossey building, with all the zoology and biology shit," he told me. "I found the parking lot closest to it, so you don't need to walk across campus."

Wow, colour me surprised. I smiled at him, which he just ignored as usual.

"What are you up to today?" I asked and saw his jaw clench. This could be a fun game. How many questions could I ask before he physically threw me out of the car?

"Just work, same as you," he replied with a shrug. Good lord, getting a detailed answer out of this guy was like pulling teeth.

"So, what are you working on today?" I inquired cooly, making him purse his lips. I thought for a moment that he'd just ignore me and continue staring at the road, but I guess he was just mulling out the answer.

"I'm working on quarterly numbers for two of my clients, and I'm presenting stock options to a potential client later today," he finally muttered, rolling his shoulders like it had taken a physical toll to answer me. He was saved from an immediate follow-up question because I was still trying to parse out what the fuck he'd just said to me. Quarterly numbers? Stock options? Before today he'd never given me a hint at what he actually did for a living, other than own a tattoo studio, which I felt probably wasn't that lucrative in the grand scheme of things. But this sounded legitimate, like an honest-to-goodness career.

"So you're an... accountant, then?" I hazarded a guess. Cain just smirked and shot me another quick glance.

"Sorry, were you expecting me to be a drug dealer or something more nefarious?" he asked, arching an eyebrow my way.

"Maybe a bookie, or a loan shark," I replied teasingly, getting a small chuckle out of him.

"Loan sharks have to have a lot of face-to-face meetings with their clients. I like accounting because I can do it from home and mostly via email," he replied. "I freelance mostly, and I've got a decent number of full-time clients, as well as all the extra work that comes in around tax season. It keeps us solvent, in case the other guys can't work for a bit." He shrugged. I nodded, a little dumbfounded at the amount of information he'd just given me. I felt like that was the most he'd ever said at one time.

"I guess I'll have to do my taxes this year, now that I'm living under your roof." I sighed, and he looked at me with genuine alarm. I kept a straight face for as long as I could before I burst out laughing, and he gave me a dirty look. "Don't worry, the business students have accounting fairs every year. I usually get one of them to do them for me," I explained, and he just sighed. "I'm not about to do them myself. The grant stuff is a horrible mess to sort out on my taxes."

Cain pulled into the small parking lot beside my building, stopping in front of the door. "I'll be here at 4 p.m. to get you. Will that work?" he asked, grabbing my bag out of the backseat. He set the strap over my shoulder, his fingers brushing my neck as he pulled away, and I was momentarily flustered by the gentleness of it.

"Sounds good. I'll be here." I smiled and climbed out of the car. Cain waited until I was inside the building before driving off. For such a cold and grumpy guy, he had the strangest gentle streak in him. Aside from our one steamy interaction in the kitchen when I'd first moved in, and the somewhat embarrassing afternoon he'd spent as my personal heating pad, he'd shown no genuine interest in me. Which, I guess, was better than the hostility he'd originally been feeling, so that was progress of some sort.

My day passed in a blur of numbers, my research having entered the less exciting data extraction portion of the study. I checked on all of my little spiders, who had recently been moved to a section of the lab closer to my office. The space had formerly belonged to Pete and his scorpions, but they had been removed by the department head, since his project was no longer happening. Now, only my spiders and one set of tarantulas remained. The lab was oddly silent now. I'd never noticed how the clicks of the scorpions had filled the space with ambient sound until they'd disappeared.

I kept a closer eye on the clock than usual today, since I didn't want to leave Cain waiting outside for me on our first day of this new arrangement. Sometimes I could get a little carried away when I got involved in something and lose track of time. Cain had my number so he could hypothetically text me if I didn't come out right away, but so far, none of the guys had shown any interest in using their phones. Probably because they were never more than two floors away from the only people they would be texting.

At a quarter to four, I started to pack up my things and close up my office. No one else was in today, so I shut the lights off as I left, locking the door behind me. I waited inside the set of doors overlooking the parking lot, scanning my surroundings to see if Cain had already arrived. I thought I saw him for a moment, leaning against a car smoking, but when I focused in closer, it was just some student, probably getting a nicotine fix between classes. Cain pulled up right at 4 p.m., waiting outside the door like he had when he'd dropped me off. I climbed in, shooting him a smile, and again he took my bag from me and set it in the backseat.

"How was your day?" I asked him, and I watched his jaw clench as we took off toward home. "Mine was quiet," I offered. "I spent most of it translating tables of data into usable results."

"Same, quiet," he replied, apparently not elaborating on that. I sighed and closed my eyes. Someday, I would get this idiot to talk about something willingly.

"You study spiders, right?" Cain asked suddenly, and I opened my eyes in surprise.

"Yes, black widows specifically," I replied, smiling. He chewed on that information for a few minutes, and I waited patiently to see if there would be a follow-up question, or if that was all the information he'd wanted.

"So what exactly do you study? Are you just watching them?" Cain asked, and I bit my cheek to keep from laughing. It was true, a lot of my job was just watching spiders in their tanks.

"I'm studying sexual cannibalism," I told him, and his eyebrows nearly shot into his hairline. "It's the idea that female black widows will copulate with the males and then immediately kill and eat them for the nutrients," I explained. "I'm trying to show the original reports that show black widows doing this were because of the lab conditions of the study and that female spiders in the wild, or a less confined environment, don't always kill their mate after copulating. Just when the male doesn't have enough room to escape."

"That's... wow." Cain let out a long breath. "That sounds really complicated. So then, all day you're just..."

"Trying to get spiders to have sex," I finished for him, smiling coyly. He laughed again, and I enjoyed seeing a look other than annoyance on his face.

"So why black widow spiders?" he asked with a sidelong glance.

"You can imagine how I might feel a bit of kinship toward them, given their reputation," I replied softly, fiddling with my sleeve. "I learned about them in high school, and the interest just... stuck, I guess." He nodded quietly. "But, if my hypothesis is correct, they're being unfairly judged," I told him. "It's not the female's fault. The males just need to learn when to get the hell out of the way." I smirked, and the corner of his mouth twitched.

When we arrived back at the studio, Cain once again passed me my bag from the backseat. A smile played on my lips as I followed him out of the car and up toward the building. I noticed something strange on the wall just inside the alley, and I veered off the path, moving closer to see it. The paint was still drying, and the bright yellow smudged my fingers as I touched the graffiti. I felt Cain come up behind me, observing it as well.

"Does this happen a lot?" I asked, studying the creepy-looking smiley face. The paint had been hastily applied, so the eyes were bleeding paint down the wall, giving it the macabre appearance of tears.

"We've had people tag our building before. It's nothing to worry about. Looks like bad paint anyway. I'm sure it'll come off the next time it rains." He shrugged and tugged on my elbow, motioning for me to head inside. I stared at the face once more before turning to head back inside, Cain close at my heels. For some reason, that smiley face gave me the creeps.

As soon as I opened the door, we heard screaming, and Cain stepped in front of me as we looked around, searching for the source of the noise. An older woman stumbled out of one of the studio rooms, screaming bloody murder as she barrelled toward us. Cain pushed me out of the way, and we watched as she ran out the door, nearly throwing herself down the steps in her haste.

Cain and I ran to the recently vacated room, and I nearly started screaming too when I saw Piper sprawled out on the floor. The chair had been moved and replaced with a little round table, and it appeared as though he'd been in the middle of seeing a client when... well... something had happened.

Blood was pooling out from underneath his head, and his eyes were rolled back so far they looked completely white. He was conscious—sort of. He had a large, unnatural grin on his face, as if he was frozen in a terrifying mask of laughter.

"Holy fucking mother of god..." Cain muttered, kneeling beside him and carefully rolling him over to check for wounds. I knelt opposite him, in front of Piper's face, touching my hands to his face.

"Piper?" I murmured, stroking his cheek. His eyelids flickered, and his eyes relaxed, rolling back down as he blinked rapidly. "What happened?" I asked.

"He wouldn't stop..." he whispered, sitting up so fast, Cain nearly toppled over behind him. "He took us, and he made me do things... horrible things..." he groaned, pushing his palms into his eyes. "I'm dead, aren't I?"

"Piper, you're not dead," Cain snapped. "Although it fucking looks like it. That'll be hell to clean up," he muttered, looking at the blood smeared all over the floor.

"You're alive. I'm right here with you," I added, more gently than Cain. I stroked Piper's cheek, trying to draw him back into the present. "Come back to me." His eyes met mine, and I watched the cloudy film slowly begin to dissipate as he focused on my face.

"Little spider," he moaned, grabbing me and pulling me flush against him, hugging me so tightly, his bracelets dug into my skin. "You're okay, you're alive." He let go of me just as abruptly and tugged my blouse up over my stomach, his fingers tracing over the smooth skin of my abdomen. "It hasn't happened yet..." he mumbled.

"What hasn't happened? Piper, is this about my brother again?" Cain demanded. I grabbed Piper's hand, stilling his examination of my stomach, and used Cain's distraction to tug Piper to his feet and away from the blood covering the floor. He was still coated in it, so I pulled his shirt up and over his head, using it to sop up some of the mess in his hair since it was already ruined, anyway.

"Who is your brother?" Piper asked. "Is he the smiling man?"

I paused halfway to the sink with his bloody shirt, turning back at those words. "Smiling man?" I asked.

"He's smiling, but it's not a proper smile. It never reaches his eyes," Piper explained, and Cain sighed and ran his hand through his hair.

"I need a smoke. I'll go and grab the mop so we can clean this mess up," he told us as I dropped the shirt in the sink and filled it with water so it could soak. It was probably a lost cause, but it didn't hurt to try. I swear, these men went through clothes faster than any other person I'd ever met.

"Don't leave," Piper whispered, making me jump. I hadn't heard him approach, and now he was right behind me, his hands moving up and under my shirt again, fixated with my stomach.

"I'm not going to leave Piper, don't worry," I replied, turning to face him. He looked so broken and so tired, his hair sticking up and matted with blood. His lips found mine, and I gasped against his mouth as his tongue slipped past my parted lips, kissing me with a desperate intensity.

"I can't lose you, Addy," he groaned, guiding me backward until I bumped against the wall. His hips shoved against mine, and I felt his erection rub against my core. His hands fumbled around my waist until he got my pants undone, pushing them down until they landed on the floor, my panties following soon after. He undid his own with a quick efficiency, and all at once, I felt him sliding inside of me, shocking me with his urgency.

"I can't lose you," he repeated, and I moaned as he thrust into me, wrapping my legs around his hips as he pinned me against the wall, his hands moving to grip my ass. There was none of the gentleness I was used to with Piper. This was all raw desperation, as if he would cease to exist as soon as we parted. My fingers dug into his back as I moaned, and I was sure there would be bruises on my hips tomorrow from where he was gripping me. His teeth scraped against my neck as he kissed me roughly, and I felt myself clench around him as my orgasm tore through me, leaving me breathless and limp as he continued to thrust, his own release arriving soon after.

I slid my legs down off his hips, my feet coming back to the floor as he loosened his grip on me. Piper's knees buckled, and he dropped to kneel in front of me, his head resting against my stomach as he murmured words I couldn't understand. I smoothed his hair down with my fingers, ignoring the tacky blood that stuck to my skin. He took a few shuddered breaths, and I dragged my pants back up, trying not to jostle him as I did up the buttons. Gingerly, I pulled him to his feet, getting him tucked back into his pants just in time. Cain and Wyatt burst through the door, startling me, and Piper slumped in my arms, pushing me back into the wall as I struggled to support his weight.

Wyatt was at my side immediately and helped lift Piper off of me, slinging his arm over his shoulder so he could keep him on his feet. I helped Wyatt carry Piper out of the studio and back upstairs to his room, while Cain stayed to deal with the pool of drying blood that had come from god knows where.

Piper was already out cold by the time we got him into his room, and I tucked him in gently, leaving my hand on his face for a moment before I snuck back out of the room to let him sleep.

Chapter Twenty-Three

Wyatt

Addy was worried about Piper. It was evident in the tension in her shoulders and the way she frowned whenever he left her sight. She was worried about all of us. In fact, I could feel it in her body every time my skin brushed against hers.

At her request, I'd driven her to the pharmacy this afternoon, while Cain had been on a call, and she'd picked up a bunch of vitamins and five pill organizers. When we'd gotten home, she'd spent the next hour hunched over the table, separating all the vitamins into the days of the week segments of each pill organizer. Austin and I watched her with curiosity as she took a Sharpie and wrote our names on the top of the organizers, assigning one to each of us. Addy arranged them carefully on the counter in plain sight so they wouldn't be missed.

"These have to be taken every day," she warned us, and Austin advanced on his with interest, shaking the container to make the little pills rattle around.

"Aren't these the things old people use?" I asked teasingly, wrapping my arms around her waist as she huffed at me.

"I wouldn't have to use them if you guys could remember to consume something other than beer and went out in the sunlight every once in a while. I swear my nails are going to start falling out." Addy grimaced, looking down at her hands, which were perfect in my opinion. "And Piper needs to take iron supplements if he's going to keep oozing blood," she muttered, and I gave her a gentle squeeze, pulling some of the worry out of her, until her shoulders relaxed and she leaned into my chest.

"Are you trying to make us more fertile, so we will give you strong offspring?" Austin hissed casually, and Addy's head shot up so fast it hit me in the chin, making my teeth click together.

"What?!" she squeaked. "No! I'm not trying to make you more fertile. Good lord, Austin! No, just healthy! I want you all healthy." Her face was turning the prettiest shade of pink, and Austin grinned and stalked forward, his pupils dilating like he'd found prey.

"I would make you some very strong offspring. I'm in my prime, physically and sexually," he rasped, puffing out his chest. I held in my laughter as Addy squirmed in my arms, turning an even darker shade of red.

"Austin, I've got an IUD. I'm not getting pregnant with anyone's offspring anytime soon," she replied gently, and I swear the snake boy actually pouted.

"Let's maybe wait until Piper's not having any more omens of our imminent deaths, and then we can talk about bringing a screaming newborn into the house, with cranky Cain and the dozens of snakes living in your room," I offered, smirking behind Addy's hair. Austin immediately brightened back up, nodding contentedly. Addy elbowed me in the ribs, and I squeezed her tighter, laughing as Austin went back to shaking his container of vitamins.

Honestly, I couldn't imagine any of us managing to father or help raise a baby. Cain would set fire to the nursery, Piper would forget the kid at the park one day, and I... well, my genetic makeup wouldn't be any good for a child. Austin, he meant well, but he was barely human himself, and I was pretty sure baby-proofing 101, included removing live snakes from the household. No, it would be better if we remained in a child-free zone, even after our lives were no longer in danger.

Austin eventually went upstairs, and I sat at the table and watched Addy make dinner. She'd described it as some fancy-sounding pasta dish, with a bunch of vegetables in it, since it would seem that we didn't eat enough produce for her liking. When I pointed out that now we had vitamins for that, she'd levelled such a nasty glare at me that I'd shut up quickly. Her temper was on a shorter fuse lately, and having two hot heads in the house was a little terrifying. I was looking for a chance to diffuse things a bit, when a door slammed shut nearby, and I could see her shoulders clench under her thin shirt. Cain stalked into the kitchen, a cigarette between his lips as he looked around.

Cain was going to run. I could sense it. He had this pained look on his face now, the frown permanently etched into his skin, and I had made a point to brush my hand against his one night as we were eating supper, under the guise of passing him a beer. Just as I'd thought, I'd felt guilt and hopelessness swirling through his veins, and I'd pulled out some of it—not too much, I couldn't handle those as well as I could pain—and I replaced it with Addy. More precisely, I'd replaced it with the feelings I got whenever Addy entered the room, that hopeful buzz, that edge of excitement, the crackle of electricity when she touched my skin, the need I had to touch her whenever she was nearby. If anything, that had just made him more frustrated.

His eyes narrowed at me briefly, and I watched his gaze shift to Addy, who was standing in front of the stove, point-edly ignoring him. She was busy fixing a plate for Piper, who'd been sleeping since his incident the day before, and I knew she was worried that he hadn't eaten. Cain stormed toward her, and I looked at the stairs, wondering if I should leave before the first shot was fired. I swear, they enjoyed riling each other up until one of them eventually snapped.

"Why did you leave the house without me?" he demanded, and she flipped her hair over her shoulder, rolling her eyes.

"I had to go to the pharmacy," she replied tartly, and her cheeks flushed as the burner on the stove flared up, sending a blast of heat toward her.

"You shouldn't have left the house! I'm trying to keep every-one alive, and you just decide to go shopping, consequences be damned!" I winced as he raised his voice and Addy turned, wooden spoon in hand, as she glared back at him.

"I'm not a fucking child!" she yelled back at him. "And I'm not stupid either. I had Wyatt come with me. I can't wait around for you all the damn time!" Cain clenched his fists, and Addy's wooden spoon began to smoke. She yelped and dropped it as the end burst into flames. She stomped out the flame quickly, and I jumped out of my chair and stepped between them so Addy couldn't take a swing at Cain. I put my hand on his arm and tried to pull out some of the anger he had swirling around inside his head. The anger was all directed inward, which was harder for me to grab ahold of, and it felt like I was dipping my hand in hot oil. Cain snarled and shoved me, and I gripped him harder to avoid bowling down Addy. I drew out as much of the rage as I could and shoved some nicer things back down in its place before Cain managed to shake me off.

"Enough of this bullshit!" Addy snapped. "Get out of my kitchen if you're going to wrestle like testosterone-filled apes!" She picked up her now blackened spoon and waved it at us threateningly. I watched Cain wearily as I felt his rage simmering in my chest, making me itch for the fight he'd been trying to start. The fight seemed to have left him though, and he was combing his fingers through his hair, staring at Addy with an almost bemused expression on his face. I moved back to the table and grabbed my beer, finishing it quickly.

"What if we're hungry?" Cain asked, still hovering close to Addy, ignoring the threat of the spoon.

"You should've thought of that before you stormed in here acting like a caveman," she snapped back, slapping at his hand when he tried to steal a piece out of the pan. He slipped around behind her, his hands dropping to her waist as he pressed her into the front of the stove. At least, this was better than the yelling, although, at this rate, none of us would be getting dinner.

I grabbed another beer out of the fridge, rubbing my temples as I tried to tune out their squabbling, which at least had taken on a more playful edge. I chugged the beer quickly, hoping to dull the edge of the rage that was simmering inside of me. Cain was a bottomless pit of horrible feelings. I didn't know how he managed it every single day.

Addy's sudden laughter filled the air, and a wave of that euphoric feeling she seemed to create emanated through the room, bringing with it a blissful calm that took the sting out of Cain's rolling anger. I sighed and closed my eyes, basking it in like a cat in the sunlight. Fuck vitamins. This was all I needed, right here.

Chapter Twenty-Four

Addison

The entire house was on edge for the rest of the week, like we were all waiting for the sky to fall. I made it a habit to check on Piper several times a day, no longer leaving him to his own devices. I also confiscated some of the sketchier-looking pills I found in his room, scared that he would hurt himself.

I didn't think Cain slept at all anymore, the dark circles under his eyes growing more pronounced with each passing day. We all stayed vigilant. The guys didn't venture out of the house alone, and the clients who came were all regulars since no one wanted unfamiliar people wandering inside the studio. Cain took me grocery shopping after work on Friday, having kept up his chauffeur services despite his growing exhaustion. He was as snarly as I had imagined he'd be in a public place, following me around the store with the cart, hunched over and glowering at anyone who got in our way. At one point, I had to stop him from nearly taking off a grocer's head when the poor man accidentally bumped me with a box of cabbages. I was thankful when we finally got out of there, and Cain and I sat in stony silence the rest of the way home.

We made it to the weekend without any more of Piper's episodes, but that didn't seem to reassure Cain at all. Apparently, Piper's omens or visions or whatever they were didn't exactly have a precise time estimate, so what he had seen could happen years from now, for all we knew. Nobody wanted to be the one to point that out though, since sleep-deprived Cain was somehow even more volatile than everyday Cain.

By the third week, we'd gotten our new routine down to a science. Every morning, I would get ready, check on Piper and Austin, and have my coffee with Wyatt. Cain would meet me by the door at the usual time, and we'd head down to the car together. I would always put my bag on my lap, and he would always take it off and put it in the backseat with a scowl. On the way to work, I'd pepper him with questions until he looked so annoyed he might drive us off the road, and on the way home I'd tell him about my day, whether he wanted to hear about it or not.

I enjoyed the consistency. It was comforting in a way, like nothing bad could happen to us if we just followed our normal schedule. So when Cain didn't meet me at the door Thursday morning, the hairs on the back of my neck prickled in warning. I brushed it off as superstitious nonsense ingrained in me by my grandma, settling in to wait. I waited for Cain for ten minutes and even checked to see if he'd already gotten into the car, but he wasn't there. Giving up, I left my bag at the door and headed back up to the kitchen, but only

Wyatt was there, sipping his coffee and reading something on his phone.

I walked hesitantly over to Cain's room, where the door was still shut, and I knocked tentatively. When he didn't answer, I knocked again, then quietly opened the door and peeked inside. Cain was lying in bed, shirtless and asleep, his sheets half-off and tangled around his legs. He looked sick, a sheen of sweat on his forehead, his forehead somehow furrowed even while unconscious. I watched his fist clench, and then the sheets underneath him started to smoke, like when you left an iron against the fabric too long.

"Oh shit, oh shit," I muttered, dashing over to the bed, looking for something that could put out a fire in a pinch. Of course, he didn't keep anything non-flammable nearby. That would've been too easy. I grabbed his shoulder, shaking it lightly. "Cain, wake up!" I insisted, but that didn't work. More smoke was filling the room, along with the smell of burnt fabric.

"Cain, please wake up." I bent over him, pressing my hand to his face. He was burning hot and clammy, and I wasn't sure what we would do if he was sick enough to warrant a hospital. His eyes suddenly popped open, wide and terrified, like he didn't know who I was. He moved so fast I didn't have time to react, just scream, as Cain grabbed me and pulled me down onto the bed, rolling on top of me to pin me down. His hand was at my throat, and his other made a fist, cocked like he was going to hit me.

"Cain, stop!" Wyatt grabbed Cain from behind, dragging him backward off the bed. I scrambled to my feet, watching the two men struggle on the ground. Wyatt had the upper hand, and slowly Cain settled in his arms and finally stopped trying to pull him off. Wyatt let him go only after a few minutes, both of them out of breath. The skin on Wyatt's arms was red, like he'd stuck them under hot water too long.

"Fuck, I'm sorry," Cain groaned, dropping his head into his hands. Wyatt patted him awkwardly on the back, getting to his feet gingerly.

"It's fine, man," Wyatt replied, walking back over to me. He touched my arm gently, and I realized I was shaking a little. "I'll take you to work, okay? You might want to, uh…" He touched my neck, which ached like a fresh sunburn. "I don't know if you have a scarf or anything you might want to wear?" he suggested quietly. I just nodded mutely and left the room as quickly as possible, running downstairs to the basement.

I let out a shaky breath as I checked myself out in the bathroom mirror. It might've been a first-degree burn, nothing worse than that, along my neck, just above my collarbone. Unfortunately, it was the very obvious handprint shape that would raise a lot of questions, so I opted for a less revealing outfit today. I didn't have any scarves, since working with spiders didn't really encourage loose layers, but I did have a turtleneck that would do nicely. It was a little warm for a sweater still, but I could pull it off without anyone being too suspicious. With the burn now covered up, I ran back upstairs to grab my bag, Wyatt already waiting by the door.

We climbed into the car in silence, and it was only when we were on the road that Wyatt finally spoke up. "I know that was horrible, and you have every right to be mad," he told me quietly. "But you need to know that he wouldn't hurt you on purpose, or any of us, for that matter." I absorbed his statement, chewing my lip.

"So, that has happened before?" I asked finally. "He just goes crazy?"

Wyatt grimaced. "The best I can figure is it's a side effect of a traumatic brain injury he had when he was a kid. We don't know because he'd never go into an MRI willingly. Think of it like a PTSD flashback, but because Cain is... well, Cain, they're a lot more dangerous." He sighed, and I touched my neck where I could still feel the sting of the burn as it brushed against my shirt.

"How did he get hurt?" I asked quietly, but Wyatt just shook his head. "I don't know the details. All I do know is that his brother was not a good guy. He was a couple of years older than Cain, and he had something messed up in his head. You know, like those serial killers on TV," he explained. "He doesn't feel emotions like a normal person. It's like he can't have them, so he just fakes them. But he likes to hurt people, and he hurt Cain a lot." His jaw clenched, and my stomach twisted as I thought about the pain in Cain's face when he'd woken up.

"Why didn't his parents stop him? Shouldn't they have noticed something was wrong?" I demanded, horrified.

"His brother is sort of like us," Wyatt replied quietly. "More like you, though, I'd guess. He's very good at getting his way. People just listen to him and believe him. It didn't work on Cain, but it worked on his parents. His brother would tell them everything was fine, and they believed it." My stomach clenched again in disgust. Someone with that kind of power and no moral compass... that was a nightmare combination.

We pulled into the parking lot, and I clutched my bag, which I'd left sitting on my lap. Wyatt pulled out his phone and checked the time. "You can text me when you're ready, and I'll come pick you up, okay?" He smiled, but it was clearly forced. I nodded and gave him a weak smile in return, kissing him softly on the cheek before sliding out of the car.

The day went by at a snail's pace, which I didn't mind for once. I didn't feel like going home just yet, not after what had happened. I wasn't mad at Cain. It had obviously been a horrible accident and not intentional on his part. But I just wanted some time to absorb what Wyatt had told me. It did explain a lot about Cain's whole stand-offish personality. I was so wrapped up in my own thoughts that I didn't even hear when someone joined me in the lab.

"Hey, sorry to interrupt." I jumped out of my chair, nearly knocking over the tank I'd been working with. A man I hadn't seen before was standing just inside the door, his hands in his pockets.

"Sorry, yes, hi." I scrambled to collect myself, and he gave me a wry smile. "Are you looking for someone?" I asked. The other faculty member who was normally around in the afternoons had left early today. I hoped he hadn't forgotten he was meeting his TA or something.

"Something actually, I'm supposed to have an office in here?" he replied, looking around. "I'm the new researcher," he explained. "My study is on scorpions." Oh shit, a jolt of pain went through my chest. He must be Pete's replacement.

"Of course, it's just down the hall there." I pointed. "The one furthest down. It should be unlocked," I told him. He smiled gratefully and headed down the hallway.

I finished up with my subjects and settled them away on their shelves for the day, heading back to my own office to type up my notes. I'd almost forgotten about the new guy when he knocked on my door, opening it a crack. "Do you mind?" he asked, stepping in before I could answer. It was the same thing with every new person that came in. They wanted to make friends and chat, and I'd have to be nice but distant until eventually they'd get the hint and leave me alone. He walked over to the bookshelf set up against the one wall of my office, studying its contents.

"Can I help you with something?" I asked politely, but with a bit of an edge. I was tired and not in the mood to play this game today. Not answering me, he pulled a book off the shelf and flipped it open idly, thumbing through a few pages.

"I just wanted to meet my new colleague." He smirked, closing the book with a snap. "You study the spiders, right? Black widows?" He walked over to my desk but didn't sit down, just stayed looming over it, toying with my book. He and his annoying smirk were really starting to grate on my nerves.

"Yes, that's right," I replied and typed something on my computer, hoping he'd get the hint, but of course, he didn't.

"Would you say your research subject is a deeper, introspective look at who you are as a person?" he mused, still fiddling with my book. I stopped typing and looked up at him, one eyebrow raised.

"Do you know what happened to the guy who used to be in the office I'm in?" he asked, switching topics abruptly. I bristled and looked back at my computer screen, quickly coming to the end of my patience.

"He passed away," I bit out, pursing my lips to avoid snapping something nasty when he perched himself on my desk, sitting on top of the notebook I was currently working in.

"That's right, he killed himself," he mused, brow furrowing. I let the silence draw out. But he didn't move from his new spot, examining the book in his hand like he hadn't noticed the palpable chill that had filled the room.

"Well, I have a lot to get done before I head home," I announced, staring pointedly at the door, but this man was the most oblivious person I had ever met.

"Your boyfriend picking you up?" he asked, smirking at me again. Okay, what the fuck was this guy's deal?

"Alright, I'd really appreciate it if you could head back to your own office now," I told him sharply, standing to emphasize my point. He just looked amused.

"You want me to stay," he replied flatly, checking his watch. My mouth dropped open at the fucking audacity of this guy. Sure, he was attractive enough, I guess, but he had a bit too much frat guy energy for my liking. He looked like a guy who would brag about his car and his stock portfolio but couldn't find your G-spot if it bit him in the dick.

"If you won't leave, I'll call campus security, and they will make you," I snapped. "Then I'll call your department head and tell him he needs to find you a new place to work." I grabbed my phone off my desk to show I wasn't fucking around.

His eyebrows popped up in mild surprise, then he chuckled softly. "It's been a while since I've had a challenge," he mused, standing up. I only got two numbers dialled before everything went black.

Chapter Twenty-Five

Wyatt

I rescheduled my last client of the day so I could swing by the campus to pick up Addy from work. Cain had been holed up in his room all day, and I knew he was beating himself up pretty good for what had happened.

Honestly, I was just surprised it hadn't been worse. I'd seen the guy melt tiles into steaming piles of goo. The fact that Addy was still alive and not in the ICU right now was nothing short of a miracle. But I was sure Cain didn't see it that way. I'd warned Austin and Piper to leave him alone for the day, and I'd done the same. I wasn't expecting to see him for at least another forty-eight hours based on the last time this had happened, which was why I was so shocked when he met me at the car at 3:50 p.m.

"Do you think this is a good idea?" I asked him as he slid into the passenger seat.

"Just fucking drive," he muttered, slouching in the seat, a cigarette already between his lips.

His sunny attitude made for a somewhat tense car ride, and when we pulled up to the front door, I finally had to say something. "She might need a bit of time," I warned him. I didn't like the idea of surprising her with him at her work, when she was only expecting me.

"I need to apologize in person," he snapped, staring out the window at the doors, watching for her.

"I know, but maybe we should wait until we get home to do that," I replied carefully. He settled on ignoring me, so we just watched the door and waited.

At 4:10 p.m. I checked my phone, making sure I had the right time. "Is she late often?" I asked Cain when I didn't see any new messages from Addy.

He shook his head, and I groaned when he jumped out of the car and stormed up to the building. I turned the car off and ran after him, hoping we wouldn't get towed for my very illegal parking job. Quickly, I followed him down the hallway, students dodging out of his way as he strode past several classrooms and what looked like labs to me, ignoring them all as he focused on his intended target. I didn't ask him how he knew where Addy's lab was. He just seemed to know these sorts of things. I nearly ran into his back when he finally stopped in front of the right lab. He tried the door, but it was locked with some sort of key card scanner. Looking around us quickly, Cain peered through the small window on the door, cupping his hand to see through the glass.

"Fuck!" he snarled, startling me, and he grabbed the handle again. This time the metal started to glow hot, and the electrical panel fizzled and popped, the door opening with a swift jerk. Oh fuck, we were going to get arrested for sure. I followed after Cain as he stalked inside the room, shutting the door to make it look less obvious we'd broken in, although the smoking and melted door handle was a bit noticeable.

I didn't know what labs normally looked like, but I assumed they were usually cleaner than this. Glass littered the floor, and tanks were shattered across the room. My heart started to pound, and I followed Cain toward the rooms at the back of the lab. One of them had to be Addy's office. I saw her purse on the floor, along with something that looked eerily like blood, and a damaged book that had been tossed aside.

"Motherfucker," Cain growled. I followed his gaze to see Addy's phone on the desk, along with a pile of dead spiders arranged in a macabre approximation of a smiley face.

"Is it... him?" I asked, but I already knew the answer. Cain turned and stormed off without saying another word. I quickly grabbed Addy's purse and her phone, stuffing them in my hoodie as I ran out after him. I had barely gotten in the car before Cain was peeling out of the parking lot, and I hurriedly put on my seatbelt as Cain drove us home.

I dug through Addy's purse to see if there was anything unusual left behind, but found nothing useful. I turned on her phone, which was password-protected, and I swore under my breath.

"Try 1106," Cain snapped, his eyes focused on the road. I rolled my eyes and typed in the numbers, but sure enough, it worked. "It's her birthday," he muttered when he noticed me glaring at him. I started clicking through her phone random-ly, trying to find anything useful. I clicked on her photos app and my blood ran cold. There were pictures taken from this afternoon on her phone, but it was obvious that Addy hadn't been the one who'd taken them. One was a photo of her lying on the floor of her office, blood running down the side of her face. The second photo was somehow worse, a close-up of her unconscious face with some guy's face pressed up beside it like a fucked-up selfie.

"Is this your brother?" I demanded through gritted teeth, holding the phone out for Cain to see. That was my mistake, and I regretted it as we swerved violently into oncoming traffic, receiving several angry honks from other drivers on the road.

"I'll take that as a yes," I muttered, stowing the phone as Cain unleashed a violent, unholy torrent of curse words, slamming his fist into the dashboard. Each hit left a smoking dent in the poor car, and I was just thankful to be in one piece by the time we got home. Austin and Piper were in the kitchen when we got inside. Piper looked pretty rough. His eyes were glazed over again, and his head was bleeding in a chilling imitation of the photo on Addy's phone.

"I heard him screaming and found him like this," Austin rasped, his eyes wide. "I don't know what happened, but I think he hit his head on something, he's not making any sense." Cain stalked past him, and I thought for a second that he was just going to leave us here in the kitchen. But he was just pacing, running his hands through his hair tiredly.

"Smoke, choking smoke. My head hurts. I'm really cold," Piper mumbled, shaking his head dazedly. "It's cold, and I'm alone, but not alone. He's got puppets with his crooked smile, and they're hurting me and hurting themselves. He just wants to laugh and make us dance on strings. So many strings..." He looked up at the ceiling, looking at the invisible strings. I frowned and crouched beside him, playing his words over in my head to try to find some meaning in them.

"Where are you?" I asked Piper, and his eyes scanned the room, but not the one we were in. "Can you describe it?"

"It's cold and damp. Darkened, busted windows surrounded in concrete, old concrete, smells like mould. There's a train that rumbles the walls and shakes the floor, and seagulls are screeching. Nobody can hear me if I scream," Piper whispered, shivering. His lips were a blueish tinge, and his wrists started weeping blood from wounds that weren't there.

"Cain... I think he knows where Addy is," I murmured, and Cain stopped pacing, stalking toward us. Piper looked over at him, eyes unfocused but fixed on Cain at the same time.

"Where's Addy?" Austin asked us, looking alarmed, but I ignored him for the moment, focusing on Piper's rambling.

"He wants you weak... he's using her as bait... people are his shields... he can't control us like he controls them... he wants to hurt you!" The words came out in great bursts of air, and Piper's face twisted in pain as he screamed so loudly we all covered our ears. Piper finally slumped over in the chair, nearly tumbling right out of it. I managed to catch him by his shoulders and propped him back up gingerly. Cain swore again and resumed his pacing, while Austin hovered beside me anxiously.

"Where's Addy?" he asked again, pulling at my shoulder. Once I was sure Piper wouldn't crash to the floor, I stood up, rubbing my hand over my face.

"Cain's brother took her, we don't know where she is." I sighed. Austin's face twisted in pain like I had slapped him. He started shaking his head, looking at Cain like he'd correct me and say it was just a joke. Cain was too busy pacing and swearing to be much comfort. His hands were smoking and small burn holes were popping up all over his shirt as he walked.

"You'll find her, right?" Austin rasped, looking at me with desperate eyes. I opened my mouth to offer something, anything, that could comfort him, but I had nothing. His eyes narrowed at me, then at Cain. "Find her!" he hissed, his voice cracking when he tried to raise it above his usual whisper.

"We're going to try Austin, I swear. I just - we just don't know where to even start." I grimaced. This didn't seem to help much, and his fists were clenched in rage.

"Find her!" Austin snarled, his voice nearly unintelligible now, more a hiss than actual human speech. I heard something move upstairs, and after a quick headcount, I realized that no one should've been up there right now. I started for the stairs but backtracked immediately when a snake appeared, barreling toward me. It continued past the kitchen and down the stairs. I looked back at Austin, who was still hissing or muttering or doing something with a significant amount of concentration. Another snake slithered past, then another, and I leaped away from the stairs as dozens of snakes started to cascade past us in a brown and green waterfall.

Even Cain stopped pacing for that, his eyes widening in shock. "Did... you know he had that many snakes in the house?" I asked him quietly. Cain shook his head. Okay, great, well, I would definitely be checking my room every night before I went to sleep from now on. We watched as close to a hundred snakes slithered past us, down the stairs, and when the stampede—could snakes stampede?—finally died down, I whirled on Austin. He looked tired now, and the little red snake that was normally curled around his arm had travelled up to circle his neck, its tongue poking out and testing the surrounding air.

"We'll find her," he mumbled, finally in a language I understood. "We can smell her, so we can find her." I patted him on the shoulder, and he sat down, putting his head in his hands. I checked to see if Piper was still breathing, and he was, but shallowly, tears staining his cheeks. Cain resumed his pacing, his shirt smoking as more holes burnt through it. It had only been a few hours, and we were already falling to pieces. What would happen if we didn't find her soon?

Everyone, including myself, was concerned about Addy and how to get her back. I couldn't help but wonder how bad it would get if we didn't get to her quickly enough. Normal people seemed to have a near-immediate withdrawal, losing their minds within days of losing her. What would happen to us? We were already so fragile. Could we hold it together long enough to save her?

Chapter Twenty-Six

Austin

It was so quiet up here now with most of my friends gone. I curled up on my bed, my little red-bellied snake still wrapped around my neck for comfort. She was too small and too young to go outside, and she knew she was of better use here with me, anyway. Cain said I couldn't go out to look for Addy, and I'd snarled at him for that rule. My friends were currently searching all over the city for her, and I told them to look in chilly places, near seagulls, concrete and trains. That was what Piper kept repeating, his eyes unfocused and haunted as he mumbled the words over and over. My friends would smell for her, but they wouldn't be able to save her. You needed hands for saving, so we could only search and report. We couldn't do anything else.

I snarled and rolled on my bed, scratching at my arms. It was too quiet now, with the den empty. I missed the warmth of my friends and the comfort of their sounds in the night. I rolled off my bed with a sigh, the floor biting-cold on my skin. Dropping to my stomach, I pulled myself under the bed, where it was dark and cozy. I curled up in the darkness, my little red snake hissing gently in my ear. My skin felt too tight, but I was too human to shed it like my friends. I scratched at my arm, trying to relieve the itch that was growing, but it didn't help, even when I drew blood, my nails digging too deep into my flesh. My friends would find her, they had to find her.

I fell into a restless sleep and dreamed of Addy's face and the feel of her skin against mine. She was perfect, my Addy, and I needed her back. I knew snakes didn't normally mate like humans did, but my humans didn't seem to want to mate like most humans, anyway. I didn't understand weddings, where two people signed a paper and said they wouldn't fuck anyone else forever. You didn't need to sign a paper to love someone; I didn't think. No other species did that, and there was plenty of love in the world. Cain told me once that marriage was for tax purposes, but I didn't do taxes, so that didn't apply to me, either. I had a bond with Addy just like I had a bond with my friends, so we would stay together forever. If she wanted a piece of paper, I was sure one of the guys would get her one. They'd know where to find them. And if she wanted offspring, I would build her the best nesting space I could manage with my bare hands. She would want for nothing, and I would die for her.

My chest ached, and I curled inward, pain slicing through my core, waking me from my doze. We'd already let her get taken away. We were too weak to protect her. If Cain couldn't protect her, then how could I? I wasn't a worthy mate. She needed someone strong. A low keen escaped my throat, and

I rolled again and again, trying to smother the burning itch in my skin. I couldn't stop scratching, it was hurting too much.

I was not sure if I dozed, or if I slipped into unconsciousness. It was hard to tell if time was moving in the silence of my den. I heard Cain cursing from somewhere below, and the house creaked in protest, my window rattling as thuds sounded through the walls. Little Red poked her nose up, tasting the air. She slipped down from my neck, coiling wildly around my wrist, forcing me out from under the bed. I stumbled for the window, the light blinding me through the crack in the newspapers coating the glass. I wrenched the window open an inch and stared mutely as three of my little friends slithered inside, coiling around me immediately for warmth. I winced as their scales brushed the fresh scratches on my skin, trying to listen as they described their adventures.

Addy wasn't on the busy street by our studio, and she wasn't near the campus, or down by the river valley. I heaved a sigh, leaving my window cracked and curling back up with my friends under the bed. They slithered and hissed, trying to comfort me as we waited for news from the others. The itch under my skin grew as we waited. I tried not to scratch, but my hands moved on their own while I dozed, and I'd wake to find fresh marks on my arms and legs.

Steadily, my friends returned, all hissing mournfully as they reported the bad news. Addy wasn't near the east-end train tracks, or by the tunnels. Addy wasn't sensed near the sewers, or in the dense cluster of buildings on the north side. My den hummed with life as more and more bodies returned, everyone as restless as I was, waiting for information. At some point, the house creaked with Wyatt's steps, and I heard my door open. I didn't want to see anyone right now, so my friends who were nearest to the door told him to leave. I heard him curse and shut the door quickly, and I returned to my doze, scratching my neck to soothe the pain under my skin.

It was late, or maybe early, when more of my friends returned home. Downtown had been searched thoroughly, but Addy wasn't sensed near any of the tall buildings that lived there. My friends, who'd searched the river valley on the west side, also reported no sign of her. I was beginning to despair. If Addy had been taken out of the city, we would never be able to find her. My body was covered in a blanket of scales, bodies shifting and settling over me, as I searched for a bare patch of skin to scratch. It was getting louder in my room again, the den nearly full to its typical capacity, but I still felt painfully alone.

I couldn't tell what day it was, or what time it was anymore. I couldn't see the light from my window from under the bed, so there was no way to tell if I was sleeping or awake. The itch was all I could think about. My skin was stretched so tight I thought it would tear if I moved. A wave of hissing travelled across the room, everyone stirring at once as if someone had disturbed them. I blinked open one eye, then the other, listening as the sound rose into a cacophony of hissing.

My garter snake friend slithered through the masses, coiling around my neck in a frenzy. I sat up too quickly, smashing my head against the bottom of the bed, and I rolled onto my stomach so I could crawl out from underneath the bed. My friends cleared a path for me to stumble to the door, the garter snake on my neck still hissing against my ear.

I stumbled down the stairs, my legs weak from being curled up for so long. Wyatt was in the kitchen, asleep on the table, an open laptop next to his head. I knocked into his chair on my way past, steadying myself against the wall. I needed to get to Cain's room right away.

"Austin, are you okay?" Wyatt asked from behind me. I barged into Cain's room, catching him off guard. He was sitting at his desk, busy on his laptop, and he looked up at me with a scowl that morphed into shock.

"What the fuck happened to you?" he snapped, standing quickly. I bared my teeth at him, hissing, and he stopped short. I heard Wyatt come up behind me, and my friend hissed a warning at him, too.

"Addy is by the docks," I rasped, my voice struggling with the sounds. "An old warehouse, with red on the outside, right on the water." Cain just stared at me, his eyes wide.

"We saw her there! At the docks!" I insisted, my voice cracking with the effort of yelling. Why was he just standing there? We needed to go!

Cain put up his hands, walking slowly toward me like he was afraid I would bite him. "Okay, Austin, thank you. We'll go check it out." He walked past me like that was that. I struck out, gripping his arm tightly. "I'm coming too," I told him in a low voice.

"No, you aren't. You're staying here," Cain snapped, wrenching his arm away. "You're in no condition to go any-where." I snarled at him, and Wyatt stepped between us quickly.

"Austin, look at yourself, man. You can't go anywhere like this," he murmured, and I stopped, confused. I looked down at my body, my breath catching in my chest. My skin was in ribbons, deep red grooves carved all over every inch of my skin. Some were still weeping blood, and others were scabbed and peeling, exposing blue-green scales under-neath. The itching was so bad, I wanted to tear my skin off completely. I whimpered, looking back at Wyatt. He looked as bad as I felt, his face pale and sickly, with dark purple bruises forming under both his eyes. "Cain and I will go and get her, okay? You need to stay with Piper."

Nodding dully, my gaze dropped to the floor. I was weak. I couldn't help her right now. Wyatt patted my shoulder gently, and I felt myself settle, the itch easing up just a bit. His own face became pinched, and I knew he'd helped me in his way. "You did good man, you found her when we couldn't," he told me, and I lifted my head a little. He gave my shoulder a squeeze, then turned to chase after Cain, who was already headed to the car.

I listened as the car tore away from the building, the house growing silent once more. My eyes were heavy, now that my skin had stopped itching as badly, and I trudged back up the stairs. I was stuck waiting again, uselessly, which made my chest ache. I curled back up under my bed, my friends enveloping me back into the darkness.

Chapter Twenty-Seven

Addison

I didn't know what woke me up first, the train horn as it rumbled past, shaking the ground underneath me, or my own teeth chattering from the cold. I tucked my knees up into my chest, trying to conserve my warmth. My fingers brushed against the skin of my legs, which was weird because I had been wearing pants. Wait, why was I on the ground? I forced my eyes open, blinking as they adjusted in the dim light. I looked down at my hands, which were tied together with a weird nylon-type rope. Panic blossomed into dread, as I tried to fill in the blanks in my memory that would explain why I was tied up in a warehouse, wearing only my underwear.

I sat up, tucking my legs into my chest to keep warm while I worked on the rope around my wrists. The material was some horrible synthetic blend that wouldn't fray even when I chewed on it, and trying to loosen it only made my wrists raw. Failing at freeing myself, I started to look around the room, searching for something that I could use to cut myself free or cut up whoever had fucking done this to me. I stood up gingerly, my leg sore from lying on the freezing concrete for so long. There was some promising trash piled up near one window, so I began to make my way over there, dragging the rope behind me as I stepped carefully over any jagged-looking rocks. I needed to find something sharp enough to cut a rope, not stab myself in the foot.

I'd nearly made it to the edge of the pile when the rope pulled tight against my wrists, yanking me backward with a jerk. I stumbled, trying to keep my footing as it pulled me back to where I'd been laying, continuing its journey upward, toward some sort of pulley-hook thing in the ceiling. My arms stretched painfully tight over my head, as I was lifted into the air, my toes just able to touch the floor if I strained hard enough. Someone chuckled and stepped out of the shadows, and I recognized the jackass from the lab. I glared at him, yanking on the rope in hopes it would magically unravel so I could strangle him with it.

"I'm impressed," he mused, walking around me in a lazy circle. "Most people have a few minutes of terror, or even a little crying session, before they start trying to escape. That's one of my favorite bits." He sighed, finally stopping in front of me, but leaving enough room so I couldn't do anything nasty, like spit at him, which I'd considered.

"Who the fuck are you?!" I snapped, swaying slightly as I lost my footing. I stretched my toes down to stabilize myself, my arms already burning from holding my weight on their own. He watched me struggle with mild interest, as if he was conducting a study and I was the subject.

"My little brother didn't tell you about me?" He cocked an eyebrow. "I feel like sharing big family secrets would make for some prime pillow talk, but I guess Cain was never good at opening up to people," he mused. "I'm Jacob, but you can call me Jake since we're going to become close friends." He smiled. "Do you prefer Addison or Addy? I think I like Addison. It's got a sultry sound to it."

Ew, what is with this fucking guy? "Okay, Jake," I replied coldly. "Let me go, and you can call me whatever the fuck you want." I twisted my wrists, pulling at the rope, wishing for even a centimetre of give to take some of the pressure off my aching shoulders.

"You're quick. I like that," Jake announced, circling me again. He reminded me of a shark with his cold, dead eyes. Even when he smiled, they never changed. It was as if he was doing a creepy pantomime of emotions instead of actually feeling them. "I can see why Cain keeps you around. You're not bad to look at either," he told me, and I scowled at him. His roving eyes made me want to put on extra layers of clothes. "It's too bad about that." He sighed, flicking his fingers to my old burn scars across my shoulder and my collarbone. "I bet Cain liked those, though."

"Cain is letting me crash at his place for a while, that's it," I snapped at him. "But you should really talk to someone about your creepy obsession with your brother's sex life." He chuckled and shook his head, taking a few steps closer.

"Really? So you'd normally let a roommate leave a hand-print on your neck?" he asked, staring at the mark Cain had made. My cheeks heated, and he looked annoyingly smug. "I'm sure he just needed to mark his territory. I bet you have your hands right full with all those horny little freaks in that dump he calls home." My toes were cramping with the effort of holding myself up, and I could feel sweat beginning to run down my back from the strain on my arms.

"Just tell me what the fuck you want already!" I yelled at him, and he smiled, watching my feet shake as I struggled to balance on my tiptoes.

"I want to understand you, that's all." Jake grinned. "So I can figure out why my brother likes you so much. I know you're different. Don't bother with the whole denial thing. I saw the file on your little lab buddy Peter, and I dug into your past. You're quite the naughty girl." He started to circle around me again, and I hated when he went behind me and I couldn't keep my eye on him. It was like turning my back on a wild animal. "What exactly do you do to people to make them so... crazy?" he asked, pacing back in front of me.

"Why don't you come closer and find out for yourself?" I snarled, making him laugh.

"Believe me, I'm horribly tempted." Jake sighed, moving closer but still just out of lunging distance. "The thought of something so addictive it makes you lose your mind, well it's truly hard to resist. But I'm no dummy. I never try anything without seeing what it does to someone else." He smiled. "That's why I brought a friend." My stomach clenched in fear as he called someone else out of the shadows. His 'friend' was an older guy, scruffy and slightly overweight. He looked like one of the dock workers. He probably worked in the area.

"Go over and touch her," Jake told his friend, slapping him on the back. I twisted and tugged against the rope, scraping the skin off my wrists, but I couldn't get away from the enormous stranger lumbering toward me. He had a stupid look on his face, like he had been smacked over the head with something and hadn't quite recovered. The second his hand brushed my waist, I saw his look shift, his eyes glazing over.

"Get away from me!" I snapped at him, and he immediately dropped his hand and backed away from me. Jake looked thrilled by this, which I wasn't expecting.

"Excellent!" he announced, rubbing his hands together. "What else can you do to them? How much power do you have, exactly?" he asked. When I didn't answer, he just looked back at his friend. "Touch her again," he ordered. The man looked torn for half a second before stalking over again. This time, when he touched me, I had a better plan.

"Run and call the police!" I shouted at him, and he turned to bolt from the room. A small bubble of hope formed in my chest.

"Stop." One word from Jake, and the man immediately froze, popping my bubble. Jake turned to frown at me, like I'd just hurt his feelings with my escape attempt. "Play nice," he warned me. "Or I won't play nice with you." He pulled a knife out of his pocket, flicking it open. "Now, he's going to touch you for a few minutes, so I can see what happens when it wears off. If you tell him to run again, I'll hurt him, and then I'll hurt you, understand?"

I glared at him, my lip curling in disgust. He took my silence as a yes and ordered his friend back over. "Touch her," he snapped, and the man's hands were on me again. I bit my lip to keep quiet as his hands moved over my body, cringing away when he started to get more interested in it, his hands moving over my breasts. "Alright that's enough for now. Step away," Jake announced, and I let out a shaky breath. My arms were screaming in pain, and blood was starting to trickle down them from the raw wounds on my wrists.

"Well now, I guess we just wait and see." he mused. I watched, my eyes hazy with pain and rage, as he got some more rope and tied his large friend to the wall closest to me. The guy sat quietly, not moving or even speaking, and Jake looked satisfied with his handiwork. He walked over to where he'd left his bag and pulled out something that looked like a syringe. "I like you feisty, but I'd hate for you to escape while I'm gone, so I'm going to give you a little something to make you more comfortable," he told me, and I immediately began to kick and flail as he approached me. My body spun as I lost my footing, and he took the opportunity to jab the needle into my neck. I felt a cool burn as whatever was in the needle spread into my bloodstream, and my muscles went slack as all of my energy disappeared. "I hope you two enjoy yourselves. Don't worry, I'll be back in the morning." He smiled, and I spat at him weakly as he walked away.

I felt the rope jerk against my wrists, and I dropped abruptly to the floor, my legs too weak to catch me. It was not a graceful fall. I landed in a heap and immediately curled up in a ball, tucking my arms down against my chest. I stared at the man across from me, but he looked almost lifeless, with no thoughts or function behind his eyes. He hadn't moved since Jake had left. The only way I knew he was alive was the occasional blink and the rise and fall of his chest.

My vision faded around the edges and I turned my head to look out into the darkness, tears sliding down my cheeks. I'd started shivering again, the chilly night air seeping in through the broken windows. I could hear the sounds of the night all around us. The birds had quieted down, but a coyote was howling nearby, and I thought I could hear the sound of frogs drifting up from the water. Something rustled nearby, and I had a horrible vision of having to fight off rats on top of everything else right now. I saw a brief flash of movement in the dark, a small shape close to the ground. I stayed very still until I spotted a long shape sliding across the floor.

A little snake slithered toward me, stopping to test the air with its tongue. It could easily be a coincidence. There was a lot of wildlife around the docks, after all. But something about this snake felt a little too... deliberate to be pure chance. "Tell him I'm here, okay?" I whispered to it, and it disappeared in a flash. I doubted very much that it had understood me, but if I didn't have hope, I might just lose my mind.

I curled up as tightly as I could, shivering as the night grew colder. At some point, I guess I must've drifted off to sleep. The drugs he'd given me weakening my body to a point of exhaustion, where even the fear of being eaten by rats couldn't keep me awake.

Chapter Twenty-Eight

Addison

I woke to a horrible squelching sound, and my stomach immediately turned. I jolted up when I heard it again, wincing as my shoulders screamed in protest. The ropes around my wrists were stained a horrible brown from my blood, and my skin underneath was mottled and puffy. I looked around for the source of the sound, turning to check on Jake's zombie friend, and zombie seemed to be the apt description. He had evidently been struggling to free himself while I'd been asleep, and when he couldn't get the ropes off his wrists, he'd decided to just chew his hand off, like some kind of feral coyote caught in a trap.

I turned away just as he ripped another chunk out of his arm, the blood making a horrible splattering sound across the floor. "Isn't it just fascinating?" Jake announced, making me jump. He was seated in a folding chair, watching the guy chew his own wrist off as if it was an afternoon Little League match. Jake got up and walked away for a moment, and I cried out in pain as my arms were wrenched upwards, dragging me up to stand. He left me just a little more slack today, so I could nearly stand on the balls of my feet if I tried. The pain made me dizzy for a bit, and Jake clapped his hands in front of me impatiently to get my attention.

"Come on now," he told me. "This is the good stuff right here. Watch this now." He walked over to the man, who seemed to not even notice he was there. "Stop that," Jake told him, and the man immediately dropped his arms, blood still trickling down his chin. "Tell me, what do you need?" he asked him.

"I need to get to her," the man replied, his voice flat and robotic. His eyes focused on me, and it was like all the sanity had bled out of him overnight.

"Tell me, why do you need to get to her?" Jake asked, looking at me like I should be excited by this horror-show experiment.

The man's face went pained, and he reached toward me with his bound hands. "She's everything, all I can think about. I need her. I would do anything to be with her."

"Fascinating," Jake murmured. "Alright then, as you were," he told him, turning away from him. The man quickly returned to his mission, and I grimaced as the sound of tearing flesh resumed. "You have quite the appeal, it seems," he said to me, circling me again. "I wonder if my brother and his little freak friends are chewing off their limbs already. Although, I get the sense that we might be affected differently than the dull folks." He circled closer, his fingers dancing out, not quite touching me.

"I can't begin to tell you how tempting it is." Jake sighed. "I wonder what it feels like. Is it like the need for a good glass of wine with the right meal? Or is it more like heroin, I wonder. I guess if it was that good, I could just keep you," he offered, and I curled my lip at him. "Trust me, it would be miles above what Cain can give you. I can have anything I want." He laughed, holding out his arms. He really thought he was some kind of God, I realized, watching him gloat.

"Not even if hell froze over," I snapped at him, and his face dropped into a scowl.

"I guess I should've been more clear. I can have anything I want," he told me, enunciating each word as he moved toward me. "You'll learn to appreciate that." He smirked, running his finger down the side of my face. I watched his pupils dilate, and he inhaled sharply, pressing harder into my jaw. His hand dropped to wrap around my throat, and I stiffened as he started to squeeze, but he stopped there, for now at least. "Wow, that is something," he murmured. I moved my face away from him as he pressed closer, but he grabbed my chin and forced me to still so he could kiss me. His lips were stiff, the kiss as dispassionate as everything else he seemed to do. He tried to deepen the kiss, his tongue forcing its way between my lips, so I bit him, hard. Jake stumbled back, cursing, and I smirked at him.

He touched his lip, staring at the blood on his fingers like he'd never seen anything like it before. I spat out the blood I'd gotten in my mouth, snarling at him. "Well, we'll have to work on that." He sighed and backhanded me across the face. I saw stars for a minute, feeling more blood fill up my mouth. I sagged against the ropes which made my wrists burn, pulling me back into the moment as the pain cleared my head.

"It's funny. Even hurting you felt so much better than it usually does." He smirked, wiping blood off his lip. I flinched when he reached for me again, but he only ran his finger along my side, lingering on my hip. I shifted away from his hands, and he laughed again. "You fight even when you've got nowhere to go. You really are something, aren't you? I think I'll leave you with my friend again tonight. Let's see what happens if he manages to get free, shall we?" He chuckled, walking toward the door. He pulled out another syringe, and I struggled desperately, tears escaping as he stabbed the needle into my neck once again.

I looked at the feral man in the corner, still chewing at his wrist determinedly, and stifled a whimper as the drugs made my body weak. At least, I managed to catch myself this time when he lowered me down, and I sank slowly to the floor instead of crashing down, my arms sagging as the blood rushed back to my hands. I shifted as far away as I could from the crazy zombie man, laying down with my back to the far wall so I could keep an eye on him. My stomach was starting to cramp with hunger, and my throat felt dry. I had probably another day of this left in me before I started to crack, and I think Jake could probably do this forever unless he got bored, in which case he'd probably just kill me and move on to hunting puppies for sport, or whatever else psychopaths like him did as a hobby.

I shivered, dozing off but never fully sleeping in case the man managed to get all the way through his hand. At this point, all I could really do was pray that he'd lose too much blood before that happened. I felt bad for the poor guy. He'd just been in the wrong place, at the wrong time.

The sounds of squelching and blood splattering on the floor continued for hours until he finally stopped. For one blissful moment, I hoped he'd finally passed out, but then he started to sob. I covered my ears with my hands when the sobs turned to wails, unending except for the occasional thud of his head against the wall. This continued on into the early morning, and when he finally quit making sounds, I cried in relief, hugging my arms over my chest.

I must've drifted off finally in the silence of the new day, waking with a start when my body was jerked upwards. Before I could get my bearings, my head was shoved down into freezing cold water, robbing me of all thought as shock took over. I started thrashing, but the hand that held me under was unmoving. Panic began to set in as my lungs burned with the need for air. My vision faded to black, and I felt a horrible pressure as my body sucked in water, trying to get air.

This was it. I was dying.

I felt my body hit the ground, and I heaved, water pouring out of my lungs and out onto the concrete floor beneath me. I heaved again and again, until all the water was out of my body, leaving only burning pain and exhaustion behind. Laying in a heap on the ground, I shivered as the cold air mixed with the dampness of my skin, deepening the chill until I thought I might never know warmth again. A shadow passed over me, and I felt the tip of a boot in my spine as Jake loomed over me.

"There is something about watching someone drown that's just... perfect," he mused. He walked away, and for a moment, I believed that I might get a break from his torment.

With a jolt of agony, my arms were dragged up over my head, lifting me up off the floor. This time he didn't bother to leave me any option to support myself, my feet dangling inches off the floor. It wouldn't have mattered, anyway. I was too weak to hold myself up, at this point.

Jake grabbed me by the hair at the back of my head and pulled it roughly, lifting my head so I faced him, and I gave him a dirty look before my eyes flitted over to the mess in the corner. He followed my gaze and smiled. "What a shame, hey? He just couldn't get through the bone." He shook his head, smirking when he saw the look on my face. "I don't blame him, I had a restless night myself," he told me, his fingers trailing over my cheek. "I wasn't about to chew my arm off over it or anything, but I did consider coming back for you, at least once," he mused and pressed his lips to my cheek. I tried to jerk away from him, but his grip on my hair was too strong.

"Go fuck yourself," I bit out, and he yanked on my hair, jerking my head back painfully hard.

"Here's the deal," he murmured, his fingers dragging down my body. "Be a good girl, or I'll hurt you. Trust me, you'll enjoy yourself a lot more if you don't fight me, but I'll enjoy myself either way." He chuckled and grabbed my breast, giving it a painful squeeze before letting go of me completely, letting my head fall forward. Nausea climbed up my throat, his touch making me physically ill.

"Fuck you," I replied coldly. "Just kill me and get it over with, because I won't play your stupid fucking game." He cocked his head, considering me, and he pulled his knife out, studying the blade thoughtfully.

"Or I could just break you." Jake shrugged. "I've found that everyone breaks, eventually. I can play just fine with broken toys." His eyes lit up with a feral glee that reminded me too much of the poor dead dock worker in the corner. He moved up, closer to me, tracing the blade of his knife over my skin. I closed my eyes as it bit into my flesh, burning a line of agony down my chest. Stars burst in my eyes as I struggled to stay conscious, the world going grey around the edges.

Jake studied my face, eyes raking over the tears that spilled unbidden down my cheeks. He caught one with his finger, considering it as a jeweller would assess a precious gem. I shivered as the knife shifted lower, whimpering as another wave of pain washed over me, his knife cutting a line down across my stomach. "Are you ready to behave?" he asked me softly.

"Eat dog shit and *choke* on it," I spat out, gritting my teeth. He walked around me until I could no longer see him, and my body shook even harder. My vision was tunneled. I didn't think I'd be conscious much longer. Something flashed in front of me, but before I could dwell on what it might be, the bite of metal across my shoulder blade pushed any other thoughts out of my head. I think I screamed at that point, and my head fell against my chest, too weak to hold it up anymore.

For a moment, I was suspended like that, and then the ground reached up to meet me. I landed in a heap, barely conscious. I saw Jake kneel down beside me and felt his hands as he rolled me onto my back. His breath was hot on my face, cloying and rotten, his tongue pushing into my mouth uninvited.

Rage swept through me, giving me one last burst of energy. I brought my head up, slamming my forehead against his nose. Blood spilled across my face as his nose broke against my skin, and he howled, reeling back in pain. I fell back against the ground, laughing weakly, and then a horrible lance of pain shot through my abdomen. I looked down to see his knife jutting out of my stomach, his face full of unbridled fury and hatred. Then he disappeared. I just blinked, and he was gone.

Huh, I guess wishes do come true.

CHAPTER TWENTY-NINE

Cain

We searched the fucking docks all morning, looking for the one that Austin had described, close to the water and red on the outside. Wyatt was driving while I looked, my hands burning too hot to hold the steering wheel. We hadn't asked if she was okay, or if she was even alive. We'd just taken a random tip from a fucking snake and ran out of the house.

I checked on Wyatt as we doubled back to drive through a new section of warehouses, these ones older and abandoned. His face was drawn and pinched like he was hurting, and he looked like he hadn't slept in days. I wasn't in any position to judge though, I probably looked the same or even worse. I was achy as if I had the flu, the buzzing in my temples nearly deafening. Guilt was eating me up inside, like acid burning its way through my organs. I should've been the one to drive her to work that morning, but I'd hurt her, and so she'd gone with Wyatt instead. What if he'd been there already, waiting? I would've recognized him. I could've stopped this before he'd even gotten close to her. What if I never got to apologize to her for what happened? I was going to kill Jake this time. He wouldn't get away with this anymore.

Wyatt suddenly slammed on the brakes, nearly sending me through the windshield. I swore and punched the dashboard, glaring at him. "That look red enough to you?" he asked quietly. I turned to look at the dilapidated building ahead of us, which had a bad coat of red paint slapped on it.

"Good enough," I muttered, jumping out of the car. Wyatt was right on my heels, and we stayed low once we got close, creeping over to the nearest busted-out window. I looked inside, moving around until I could see past the piles of trash stacked up against the wall. I could see my piece of shit brother walking around, twirling a knife in his hands. There was some sort of plastic storage container next to him, and it looked like it was filled with something, maybe water? My blood burned molten when I saw Addy's lifeless figure hanging from the ceiling, blood dripping down her body from a multitude of cuts.

"There's a door over on that side," Wyatt whispered, pointing around the side. I nodded, pointing in the opposite direction. We had a better chance if we came at him from two directions. Wyatt slipped away, circling the building opposite me. I ran as quickly as I could without making noise, searching for an entrance of some kind. Finally, I found a window that had been broken and left uncovered, and I pulled myself inside, landing on the floor in a low crouch. I stayed in the shadows, hiding behind debris as I approached. Jake had dropped Addy to the floor and was pawing at her while she was hardly conscious. My hands curled into fists, and I saw Wyatt's head briefly before it disappeared. He was close already.

Jake was leaning over her when he suddenly jerked backwards, blood pouring out of his face, and I broke into a run. I saw his look of fury as he stabbed Addy in the stomach, and I lunged without thinking, tackling him hard in the chest. We both went flying, and I landed half on top of him. He scrambled out from under me as I jumped to my feet, and I saw Wyatt dive for Addy beside me.

Jake stood up, smiling manically, his normally handsome face a mess of blood thanks to a very broken nose. "Hey there, little brother," he said, spitting a glob of blood at my feet. "I was just getting to know your little girlfriend. She had quite the body. You must be so proud."

I roared and swung at him, but he ducked my shot, lashing out with his knife and slicing a line down my arm. The wound sizzled, cauterizing itself before blood could leak out, and he cocked an eyebrow. "Look who's learning some new tricks." He smirked.

"Come on baby, just stay awake, okay?" I heard Wyatt say, and I turned to check on Addy. Jake took this opportunity to strike at me again, and I just barely dodged his knife. My foot hit a slick patch, and I slammed into the ground, rolling quickly to avoid another strike.

Jake was laughing, tossing the knife from one hand to the other, and I stumbled back as I got to my feet. "You're still too weak, Cain. You have a soft spot right here." He punched at his own chest. "If you'd just stop taking in strays, you could've been strong enough to beat me."

I narrowed my eyes at him, trying to keep both him and Wyatt in my sight. Wyatt looked at me, rolling up his sleeves, and nodded toward Jake. I had a sinking feeling he was about to do something really fucking dangerous. Sure enough, Wyatt put his hands on Addy's stomach, covering the stab wound, and his face contorted in pain. Fuck me, this was going to be too close.

I spun on Jake, and he mirrored my movements, keeping me in front of him. I charged at him, my hands burning hot, and swung a fist at his face. He laughed and rolled it off with his arm. But he'd forgotten the one key thing: I was the Devil, and my skin fucking burned. He yelped, dropping his knife as the skin on his arm bubbled with blisters. Wyatt lunged for him, grabbing Jake's face and pulling him down to the ground with him. Jake started to scream, a horrible blood-curdling sound. Wyatt pressed Jake to the ground, pinning him down as he pushed every last drop of Addy's pain and suffering into him. Grabbing a broken piece of furniture off the ground, I watch as it burst into flames in my hand. I tossed it into the pile of debris stacked in the corner and stared with satisfaction as it lit up, filling the air with acrid black smoke.

"Grab Addy and let's go," I told Wyatt. I didn't trust myself to touch her until I calmed down again. I stepped over my brother, who was still writhing in agony, moaning and clutching his stomach. We left out the side door Wyatt had come through and ran for the car, hearing muffled explosions as my fire found some leftover chemicals. I hopped in the driver's seat, snatching the keys out of the glove compartment where Wyatt had stashed them earlier. Wyatt set Addy down in the backseat and got in beside her, laying her head carefully on his lap. She was still almost naked and covered in blood, which wouldn't be easy to explain if we got stopped for any reason.

"Get something to cover her," I instructed him, peeling away from the burning building. He fished around the back seat for a moment before producing a stained hoodie of mine and hastily tucked it over her like a blanket. Addy's face was still too pale, and I kept watching her through the mirror until Wyatt gave me a dirty look.

"Focus on the fucking road, man, I've got her!" he snapped at me, and I readjusted the mirror quickly, driving as fast as I could without arousing suspicion. It was getting dark by the time we made it home, but I still pulled into the alley beside the building so Wyatt could take Addy in through the basement rather than through the front door. He tossed me his keys, and I unlocked the door for him, while he scooped Addy up and brought her down the stairs. I left them to go and park the car, sitting by myself for a moment to collect my thoughts.

I pulled out a cigarette and let the smoke fill my lungs as I inhaled, trying to slow the adrenaline that was still coursing through my veins. Jake had to be dead, right? I thought about him lying on the ground, the fire growing, the explosions as we'd left. Once Addy was safe, I would go back there and confirm. I'd check for the body. I needed to see his bones with my own eyes to know for sure. After finishing my smoke, I climbed out of the car and went inside, locking the door behind me.

When I got downstairs, I found everyone gathered around the makeshift room that was supposed to be Addy's private space. Wyatt had placed her on the bed, and she looked so still I was worried we might've been too late. He looked over when I walked in, his face pained. "I don't know what to do. Should we... uh... dress her?" He looked down at her body, still covered in blood and dirt, some of which was Jake's from when she'd broken his nose.

"Here, we'll put this on her for now, just to keep her warm," I told him, picking up the old hoodie he'd used to cover her off the floor. Wyatt helped me get it over her head, and it covered her enough for now. Addy could change into something she preferred when she woke up. We tucked her into her bed and then closed the little curtain wall around her to give her some privacy.

"Stay out of her bed," I told Austin sharply, and he nodded sadly, taking a seat in one of the nearby chairs instead. I grabbed a bottle of something off the bar and sat beside him, taking a long drink. I passed it to him as Wyatt and Piper sat down on the couch, and Austin passed it to Wyatt. The bottle made its way around a couple of times, as we told the guys in hushed voices what had gone down at the warehouse. Piper wasn't at all surprised by our story, and from the looks of it, he'd lived through at least some of it himself.

"That was a stupid fucking idea, by the way," I shot at Wyatt while he was taking a drink. "If I hadn't gotten Jake over to you in time..." He just shrugged, his face gaunt in the dim basement lighting.

"She was dying. I had to do something," he murmured.

"But you could've died too," I snapped, and his eyes dropped to the floor. "It was too close man, you can't do shit like that to us."

"I didn't die, though," Wyatt replied quietly. "And Addy didn't either." We all looked over at the curtain wall, and I wished she'd make a noise or do something to let us know she was okay.

One by one, the guys dropped off to sleep. Austin was curled up in his chair, and Wyatt stretched out on the couch with Piper beside him, using his legs as a pillow. I stayed awake, holding the near-empty bottle in my hands, watching over everyone as they slept.

CHAPTER THIRTY

Addison

I woke with a gasp, my hands groping at my stomach, but there was no longer a knife protruding from it. Instead, my hands met soft fabric. I was wearing a hoodie that wasn't mine. From the smell, it had to have been Cain's. I looked around, moving slowly as every nerve in my body seemed to spark with the ghost of pain. I was in my bed, somehow, which made little sense to me. The last thing I remembered was pain and blood. What had happened to Jake? He'd just vanished after he stabbed me like some sort of magic trick, and then everything had gone dark.

I shivered, still cold, even now that I was inside and off of the concrete floor. I shifted in the bed until I could swing my legs out and set them gingerly on the ground. They seemed steadier, but I still felt so damn weak. I grabbed the sheets hanging around my bed for support as I stood up. Pushing back the little curtain wall, my eyes slowly adjusted to the darkness of the basement. I could see the guys passed out around the couch, Austin curled up in a ball on the chair.

One set of eyes met mine in the darkness, a flash of ember sparking in the grey.

I walked over to Cain slowly and caught him off guard as I sat down on his lap, curling into his warmth and letting it seep into my bones. His body relaxed around mine, his arms coming around to hold me, enveloping me with his warmth. "I'm so sorry," he whispered in my ear, and I wasn't sure if he was saying sorry for the burn on my neck or for his psychotic brother, but either way, the apology wasn't really warranted.

I pressed my face into his chest, my arms wrapping around him tightly. A couple of tears slipped out, staining his shirt, and his hands moved across my back, comforting me. I sat there for a long time and started to doze in his arms. I felt Cain shift and lift me into his arms, carrying me back to my bed. Once he set me down, he moved to leave, but I grabbed his arm to stop him.

"Please stay," I whispered, and he hesitated a moment before climbing in beside me, tucking himself against my back, with his own back against the wall. His warmth radiated over me, and I closed my eyes, slipping off to sleep again. I guess if Cain did something, that made it okay for everyone else because, when I woke again later on, I found Austin tucked in beside me, his arm thrown over my hip. Cain was still pressed against my back, and it sounded like he had fallen asleep at some point, too. I noticed an extra arm across Austin's waist and saw Piper curled up against him on the other side. I stretched out my legs and brushed up against something with my foot. Looking down, toward the end of the bed, I saw Wyatt stretched out by our feet. I think I needed a bigger bed.

I hated to disturb them when they looked so peaceful, but my skin was starting to itch, and I desperately wanted a shower. As carefully as I could, I untangled myself from the pile of bodies strewn across my bed, stepping over Wyatt to slip off the end. Somehow, I managed not to wake anyone, and I crept upstairs as quietly as I could, making my way to Cain's room. I spent a long time in the shower, longer than I normally did. I scrubbed every inch of my body three times over—four if it was a place I knew Jake had touched me. I scrubbed so long, the water started to cool off and my skin turned a raw shade of pink. My wrists were swollen and bruised, but the skin wasn't open anymore. In fact, all of my injuries looked like they'd been healing for weeks already. I had a wicked scar on my stomach from the knife, and puffy pink lines were patterning my skin from where he'd cut me to ribbons, but they were all healing, at least. In the mirror, I could still see Cain's handprint on my neck, but it was starting to fade now. One of Jake's first cuts had been directly across the burn, some unconscious spite on his part, I was sure.

Feeling much cleaner now, I stepped out of the shower and grabbed a towel, heading into the bedroom, in search of a clean shirt. I jumped back, catching movement on the bed, but it was just Cain. I sighed with relief, my nerves still on edge. They probably would be for a long time now. "You should go back to sleep," I murmured, noting the dark circles etched around his eyes.

"I woke up, and you were gone again. I just needed to know you were okay." He sighed, rubbing his face. I walked over to his dresser and rummaged through it, pulling out a tee shirt that looked big enough to fit me like a short dress.

"I felt pretty grimy, so I wanted to shower," I explained, dropping my towel on the floor. Cain looked away immediately, giving me privacy, and I smiled. I thought we were well past the need for modesty at this point, especially considering I'd just been mostly naked for three days. I held onto the shirt, but left it off, walking over to Cain. He turned his face away, eyes downcast, until I grabbed his chin and pulled it back up so he was facing me. "It's okay," I told him gently. His eyes met mine, and they were so full of guilt and remorse that it made my heart ache. His hand reached up to brush against the burn he'd left on my neck, one finger tracing the line the knife had scored across it.

"I'm sorry," he said again and dropped to his knees in front of me, pressing his face into my stomach. I ran my hands through his hair, soothing him as he took a few shuddering breaths.

"It wasn't your fault," I told him, stroking his hair. "You didn't do anything wrong." He looked up at me, his face clouded in pain.

"He came here because of me," he replied hoarsely. "He hurt you because of me." I held his gaze as he stood, craning my neck up as he loomed over me. I touched his face gently, and he leaned against my hand, closing his eyes.

"Your brother hurt me because he was deranged," I countered. "And I'm okay now. I'm home and I'm safe." He sighed heavily, his hand moving to the scar on my neck once more.

"I don't think anyone is safe here," he replied quietly. I craned my neck and brushed my lips against his softly.

"Then we move," I replied, deliberately ignoring the true meaning of his words. "I would like a room with actual walls. And I'll need a bigger bed, like a king size, at least." I smiled, trailing my fingers down his arm. He smiled back, despite himself, leaning down to rest his forehead against mine.

"If you really want to stay, I'll get you whatever you want," he told me softly. "A bigger house, a bigger bed, even a room you can fill with spiders, if you want." He lifted his fingers up to my chin, brushing my skin so lightly that he was just the barest flicker of warmth.

"I don't know, my spiders might start a turf war with Austin's snakes, and then we'd have a real war zone on our hands." I laughed, angling my face toward his. Cain pressed his lips to mine. So gentle and sweet, I wasn't sure this was the same man I'd been living with for weeks now. I deepened the kiss, wrapping my arms around his neck so I could press my naked body against his. His hands moved to my waist, but he felt hesitant to touch me, like he was worried I would shatter if he pressed too hard.

I huffed and shoved Cain lightly in the chest, pushing him back onto the bed. I swallowed his protest, capturing his mouth with mine again as I moved to straddle him on the bed. His hands roamed up my thighs, moving to grab my hips as I ground against him, a low growl escaping his throat. "Take off your shirt," I ordered. He looked at me like he might object for a moment before his hands moved, and he slid his shirt up over his head. His torso was a battleground, scars of different shapes and sizes scattered across his chest and stomach. I traced a couple with my fingers as he watched me, eyes smoldering.

I undid the button of his jeans, shifting down so I could pull them off his hips. Cain started to sit up, and I pushed him back down, climbing on top of him. I could feel him through his boxers, and I rocked my hips in a teasing motion, rubbing my pussy against his length. His jaw clenched and heard the hiss of air as he exhaled through his teeth. I leaned down until my nipples brushed against his chest, kissing along his jaw. Cain's hands moved to my hips, his fingers digging in, as his self-control started to slip. I shifted down his legs and tugged off his boxers, freeing his dick, which was already hard and leaking. He groaned when I grabbed the shaft, teasing him again with a few gentle strokes.

Climbing back onto his lap, I rolled my hips, sliding up and down his length before I positioned the tip along my slick entrance. His eyes were burning into me, and heat poured into my core as I sank down onto him slowly, taking him in inch by inch. He bucked his hips, going even deeper inside me, until my hips were flush against his. I closed my eyes and rocked my hips, using him to hit just the right spot to send waves of pleasure through my body. I moaned, my hands dropping to his chest as I angled myself to get him even deeper, my pussy clamping down on his cock as the pleasure began to build with every thrust.

Cain rubbed my clit in slow circles, sending jolts of desire into the building pressure in my core. "Ride me, Addy, take what you need from me," he murmured, his voice husky with need. He toyed with my clit, his other hand gripping my hip as I rode him, increasing my tempo as my pleasure crested. I came with a loud moan, clenching around him until he was coming as well. Cain sat up again, and this time, I didn't push him away. He kissed me, deep and full of longing, his hand coming to tangle in my damp hair as he devoured me. When I came up for air, he continued to kiss my jaw and down my neck, his lips hot as they pressed against my skin.

He held me for a long time like that, keeping me warm with his body, until we eventually heard footsteps coming up the stairs. Apparently, we'd been gone long enough to draw notice. I slid off Cain's lap and pulled his shirt over my head while he pulled his pants back on. We were barely covered up when Austin burst in, Piper and Wyatt at his heels. Austin looked like he'd been mobbed by a hoard of feral cats, with deep scratches all over his face and neck and what I could see of his arms. Wyatt looked exhausted, even after nearly a day of sleep, and Piper resembled a ghost. I could tell he'd dropped a lot of weight in just the three days I'd been gone.

Austin's pupils dilated when he caught sight of me in Cain's shirt, which I realized a bit too late hardly covered what I needed it to. A little smile formed on his face, and I could almost see what he was thinking before he moved. I yelped out a laugh as he tackled me playfully onto the bed, kissing me and smiling as his hands travelled up my legs. Cain just laughed and grabbed his shirt before it got trapped under Austin, shrugging it over his head.

"Watch it, Austin, I've seen what happens to guys who get fresh with her," he warned, shooting me a wink. I laughed and swatted at Austin as his hands tickled along my stomach.

I think we were going to be okay.

Chapter Thirty-One

Cain

I kept an eye on things for a few weeks after we had burned down the building at the docks. A police investigation was opened when human remains turned up, once the fire had been put out. It was determined that a worker from one of the nearby buildings had gone inside for a discrete smoke break. Something had caught fire, and he'd gotten trapped and burned with the building. His body was found close to where the fire started, and no one else had witnessed anything different, so the case was closed. I could've rested easy after that, but then Addy revealed that there had been another man in the building with them. He'd died before we'd gotten there, just another victim of Jake's twisted games. This didn't add up, and I was beginning to feel uneasy.

I waited until the crime scene tape was removed from around the building, and one night after everyone had gone to bed, I headed out on my own. Parking a little ways away from the warehouse, I walked the rest of the way, just in case there was still surveillance around it. I used the same broken window to climb through, stepping over bits of debris as I made my way to where we'd left him.

The firefighters had made a bit of a mess of things while they were battling the blaze, so it was hard to pinpoint the exact spot where we'd been. I picked through the piles of burned trash and broken pieces of furniture, scanning the ground. It felt like it would have been pretty difficult for the police to miss a second body, even if it had gotten buried in the rubble. I found the spot where I was pretty sure Jake had been lying when we ran out, but it was empty. I scanned around the room. Maybe he'd managed to crawl somewhere else before he'd died. I widened my search, using my phone as a flashlight so I could see in the dark corners of the room. I walked toward the door we'd escaped through, and on the wall, near the bottom of the door, level to where someone's head might be if they were crawling on their stomach, was a small and sinister-looking drawing of a smiley face smeared on with blood.

Fuck. I walked out into the night, searching the darkness, but I doubted that he was still there, lying in wait for me. How had he survived? We'd beaten him. I'd left him dying in a burning building. How the fuck could he have walked away from that? I cursed, kicking at a rock in my path. I couldn't sleep, knowing he was out there. None of us were safe. I thought about Addy, and how close she'd been to dying. He'd strung her up from the fucking ceiling and bled her like an animal, all because I cared about her. We needed to leave, move to a different city, and get the fuck away from this place. I'd be more careful this time. I would do everything under a different name, and he wouldn't be able to find us again.

I trudged back to my car and slammed the door, pulling out a cigarette. I drove home with the windows open, letting the smoke trail off into the night. When I got back in, I found Addy curled up in my bed, even though I distinctly remembered seeing her head downstairs before I'd left. She'd snuck into my room a few times in the last couple of weeks, usually late at night when I was already asleep. I'd wake up to her arm wrapping around my chest, her hair tickling my face as she nuzzled against my neck. She never said why she did it, but I had a feeling that she was having nightmares and was seeking out someplace she felt safe when she woke up. I didn't mind having her nearby, her presence calming the endless torment between my temples. Stripping off my clothes, I slid into the bed beside her, wrapping my arms around her until she snuggled up against me. I liked these moments where I got her all to myself. It made it easier to just sit back and watch the others play and flirt with her during the day. I held her while she slept, unable to calm my own mind enough to drift off. I would start looking for a new place tomorrow, and we would move and start over together.

I would keep my family safe, no matter what.

To be continued…

Also by Bella Reves

The Bodyguard

Monsters in the Darkness Series
Black Widow's Bite - Book 1
Dreaming of Darkness - Book 2
King of Hearts - Book 3

Constrained Bouquet
Blossoming Dahlia - Book 1

Visit https://bellareves.com for more information.